PATHS OF DESIRE

PATHS OF DESIRE

A MYSTERY THRILLER

EMMANUEL KATTAN

Translated by Kathryn Gabinet-Kroo

EXILE
editions

Library and Archives Canada Cataloguing in Publication

Kattan, Emmanuel, 1968- [Lignes de désir. English] Paths of desire :
a mystery thriller / Emmanuel Kattan ; translated by Kathryn Gabinet-Kroo.

Translation of: Les lignes de désir. Issued in print and electronic formats.
ISBN 978-1-55096-417-2 (pbk.).--ISBN 978-1-55096-420-2 (pdf).--
ISBN 978-1-55096-418-9 (epub).--ISBN 978-1-55096-419-6 (mobi)

I. Gabinet-Kroo, Kathryn, 1953-, translator II. Title.
III. Title : Lignes de désir. English

PS8621.A68L5313 2014   C843'.6   C2014-902987-X
                                             C2014-902988-8

Translation Copyright © Exile Editions and Kathryn Gabinet-Kroo, 2014.
First published in French as *Les lignes de désir* © 2012,
Les Éditions du Boréal (Montréal, Canada). All rights reserved.

Design and Composition by Mishi Uroboros
Typeset in Fairfield and Verdana at the Moons of Jupiter Studios
Cover image by whiteisthecolor

Published by Exile Editions Ltd ~ www.ExileEditions.com
144483 Southgate Road 14–GD, Holstein, Ontario, N0G 2A0
Printed and Bound in Canada in 2014 by Imprimerie Gauvin

We acknowledge the financial collaboration with the Department of Canadian
Heritage, through the National Translation Program for Book Publishing. We also
acknowledge the Canada Council for the Arts, the Government of Canada through
the Canada Book Fund (CBF), the Ontario Arts Council, and the Ontario Media
Development Corporation, for their financial assistance toward our publishing.

Canadian Sales: The Canadian Manda Group, 165 Dufferin Street,
Toronto ON M6K 3H6   www.mandagroup.com   416 516 0911

North American and international Distribution, and U.S. Sales:
Independent Publishers Group, 814 North Franklin Street,
Chicago IL 60610   www.ipgbook.com   toll free: 1 800 888 4741

"I feel closer to God when I doubt his existence than when I believe in him."

—VANUDRINE SINHA

1

Wednesday, May 6, 2009

Daniel finally fell asleep. Despite the shaking of the bus, despite his neighbours' animated conversations, despite the thunderous horn-honking of the trucks rushing by in the left lane. When he boarded the plane, he stopped thinking entirely. He simply repeated the next steps to himself: once in Jerusalem, I'll leave my bags at the hotel and then jump into a taxi to go to the university. There, I'll meet with the assistant dean. I hope he'll have news for me.

Earlier, on the plane, he hadn't touched his meal. For the past two days, he'd eaten almost nothing. His seatmate watched him from the corner of her eye. She was perhaps in her thirties, but the long hair dyed a vibrant red, the silver hoop dangling from her right nostril and the skull-shaped ring on her index finger gave her the look of a rebellious teenager. All these details, however, were lost on Daniel, whose expression seemed to say he was somewhere far, far away.

The young woman tried to engage him in conversation. "Is this your first trip to Israel?"

He shook his head. So as not to be impolite, he added, "I was there several times when I was a child but I haven't been back since." Intrigued, the woman studied his face, as if she could learn more from his features, which were ploughed with furrows and wrinkles, than from his meager responses.

"Do you have family in Israel?" What could he possibly answer? Yes, my daughter. She has disappeared. No one knows where she is. It's been almost two weeks since I've had any news.

But why confide in this stranger? He would only manage to embarrass her. She would have stammered out some insignificant words. "I'm so sorry... I... if there's anything I can do—"

It was better to lie. "No, no family. I'm just visiting, that's all." And after a long silence, he pushed his earbuds into his ears.

Now, on the bus taking him to Jerusalem, Daniel reconsidered the conversation he'd had with the university's assistant dean, Doron Shemtov, five days earlier. He had been ready to leave the apartment and was just about to close the door when he heard the telephone ring. He was late but answered anyway, in case it was Sara. It had been over a week since he'd heard from her; she hadn't answered his emails or her telephone. Worried, Daniel had contacted the university. He learned that Sara had not been attending her classes. The next day, the assistant dean had called to tell Daniel that the security service had launched an investigation. A few days later, the police were alerted and Daniel took a flight to Jerusalem.

The bus moved ahead slowly. "Road work, always more road work, the bane of our existence!" His neighbour caught his eye and took the opportunity to share her frustration. Daniel nodded in agreement, then took his cell phone out of his pocket and called Sara again. Still no answer. Since speaking with the assistant dean, he had tried to reach his daughter dozens of times. Even on the plane, he had shut himself in the lavatory to secretly dial her number.

"I must not panic, I must not panic." He had repeated this little phrase to himself almost non-stop since leaving Montreal. It had become his compass, his haven, like a reassuring bit of music sung to a child to help him fall asleep. But despite his efforts, Daniel could not stop thinking the worst.

❋

Jerusalem, October 8, 2008
My father is Jewish. My mother is Muslim. I am both. I've lived a long time without asking myself any questions.

At home, Mama prayed every day. Sometimes she invited me to join her. She showed me how to wash my hands, then my mouth, nose, ears and feet, and I faithfully imitated all her actions. Then I knelt next to her and recited the few suras she had taught me. I never understood but I let her lead the way; I exhaled the modulations of her voice, and I, too, took pleasure in singing each word. I found in those moments a certain comfort and the consolation of a discipline. But what mattered above all else was feeling close to Mama, without having to speak to her or even having to look at her.

It was different with Papa. He celebrated all the major holidays — Yom Kippur, Rosh Hashanah, Pesach — and he loved telling me Bible stories, but religion didn't have a very important place in his life. Once, during Mama's illness, I asked him if he believed in God. He gazed at me with that tender look, a look that spoke only of the powerlessness of love, and said, "You know, Sara, God doesn't need us to believe in him. All He wants is for us to act as if He were there." That answer so disappointed me that I had a hard time holding back my tears. What I wanted was for Mama to get well. I wanted a giant "Yes." A frank and firm "Yes, God is there. He watches us, He listens to us, and He will save your mother." But Papa didn't understand what I needed. He believed in doctors, in their knowledge and their determination. He put himself entirely in their hands. I don't think I ever saw him pray, I mean really pray, with fervor, letting the words penetrate him. The rare times he took me to synagogue, he followed the progress of the service in his prayer book and showed me the proper pages, he bent his head when everyone else did, he chanted the praises and hymns like the others, but his face and voice betrayed no emotion. He was performing a duty and that was all. For Papa, God is only an idea. He's not there, He never was.

❧

9

From: Sara
To: Daniel
Subject: Jerusalem
Wednesday, October 8, 2008, 11:31 p.m.

Good evening, Papa,

I arrived safe and sound. I hardly slept on the plane, I was too excited. I started to read Elias Khoury's Gate of the Sun. You're right, it's very moving.

I have a room in the dorm on Mount Scopus. The weather is mild and I feel like I'm on vacation. Tomorrow: meeting at the registration office. Classes start next Monday. I can't wait.

I'm exhausted so I'm going to bed – hope I won't wake up at 3 a.m. I'll call you on Saturday.

Kisses,

Sara

From: Daniel
To: Sara
Subject: Jerusalem
Thursday, October 9, 2008, 7:18 a.m.

Dear Sara,

I was happy to get your message. I would have liked a call when you landed, but I thought maybe your phone wasn't working. In any case, I feel more reassured now.

Yesterday morning, after I left you at the airport, I took a walk in Parc La Fontaine. That was a bad idea. The place is overflowing with memories: it's where your mother and I used to take you to play before we moved to the place on Édouard-Montpetit. After 15 minutes, I couldn't stand it anymore so I went home.

I miss you. I'm waiting impatiently for your call.

Your loving papa

Jerusalem, October 9, 2008

This morning I went to the registration office to get my student card. The clerk, a lady in her fifties with a dour, unwelcoming face, studied my file for a long time. With knitted brows, she slowly turned the pages, examining my picture, lingering over a detail that seemed to hold her attention, taking down my passport number in a big red notebook. Then she looked up at me and suddenly her expression softened. "Do you speak Arabic?" She must have noticed my mother's name, Leila Hashim, and had decided that surely I knew at least a few words of this language. So I answered her in my best Arabic and her face immediately lit up.

You'd think she had suddenly found a long-lost cousin. She started asking me a million questions, curious to know where I was born, what I had studied. She told me she had worked at the university for more than twenty years and that she came from Tira, a village halfway between Haifa and Jerusalem. In contrast to the bitterness and fatigue of her features, her smile showed her gratitude at having been recognized. This complicity, born of nothing but a language, perhaps reminded her of some invisible connection, made even more precious because it was so fleeting and fragile.

Meanwhile, our little chat had aroused the curiosity of the other students waiting on the other side of the office. As I made my way to the exit, I could feel them looking at me, not in envy (why would they be jealous that I speak Arabic?) but with suspicion: if the clerk was showing me so much kindness and concern, it must mean that I merited some sort of special treatment, right?

The meeting left me with a bitter taste — and a measure of uneasiness, too. I felt I hadn't been honest, that I'd betrayed myself a bit. I should have explained to the lady that I am also a Jew, that I know my prayers in Hebrew, that my father used to take me to synagogue when I was little. But I'm sure she wouldn't have understood. The spell would have been broken, her expression would

11

*have hardened and I would have felt that if I tried too hard to remain
whole, she was the one who would be betrayed.*

❄

"Did you have a good trip?"

Taken aback, Daniel looked at the assistant dean. The question
seemed inappropriate, but his extreme fatigue had left him addled.
Without thinking, he replied, "Yes, thanks, I had a good trip. Everything went without a hitch."

"I'm afraid I still don't have any word about your daughter. When
did you last speak to her?"

"Almost two weeks ago."

"And since then?"

"Nothing since then... she seemed worried lately. She wasn't
calling as regularly. I blamed it on her classes and exams. And
then suddenly she stopped answering her emails. She stopped
answering her messages. The last one I got from her was dated
April 24th."

"Do you have any idea where she might be? Did she talk to you
about a trip of any kind?"

"No. I think that if she'd planned to go away, she definitely
would have let me know."

"Of course. In the meantime, we've turned the matter over to the
police. The officer in charge of the investigation established a list of
people likely to give us information about her. He'll certainly be able
to tell you more about it. In any case, he wants to talk to you as soon
as possible."

The assistant dean gave Daniel a piece of paper on which he'd
scribbled the police station's address. He raised his head and pro-
duced a brief smile. "For our part, we have put a 'missing' notice in
the university newspaper and on our website. Sara's professors and
friends are already working with the police. We'll do everything we
can to find her."

The assistant dean stood and offered his hand to Daniel. His energetic handshake was meant to be reassuring, but Daniel could not stop himself from reading the unsettling concern in the man's eyes.

※

Jerusalem, October 11, 2008
This morning, a long walk through the alleys of the Armenian Quarter. I had breakfast in the university cafeteria but then I walked out onto the terrace to enjoy the view of Jerusalem before my class. Even from so far away, I felt like I was in the centre of the city, in the midst of its narrow streets, its noises and smells.

※

Jerusalem, October 13, 2008
Last night on the way back from my classes, I took a walk through the Yemin Moshe neighbourhood. Since I was too tired to think, I let my eyes wander over the alleys that wind toward Mishkenot Sha'ananim. Not far from the Montefiore windmill, I stopped at the entrance to a synagogue. You could hear the melancholy lament of "Lecha Dodi," the song that announces the beginning of the Sabbath. I never really understood those words of love, where the man is the lover and repose is the fiancée that welcomes him. Aren't we in fact united with God through want, hardship and uncertainty? "And you shall love the Lord thy God with all thy heart and all thy soul and all thy might." Even during my most pious period, when I prayed every day that Mama would get well, I never felt close to those words. Love is what humans give to each other. But God, that's a question, the presence that I desire and about which I still know nothing. It allows my distress to dwell within it, perhaps it accepts all my doubts and anguish, but it is not love that unites us. To love, you have to exist for the other, and for God, I don't know if I've even begun to exist.

I stood listening to that sad song for a long time. Its accents, marked both by pain and hope, remained suspended in the stillness of the falling night. I almost went in. It would have been the first time in several years that I'd set foot in a synagogue. I changed my mind but it wasn't because I was afraid to confront the stares of strangers or because I would have had to go up to the women's section and stay hidden behind the wooden lattice that would keep me from seeing the prayer service. Instead it was because I feared the feelings that this rapprochement would have aroused in me.

Finding myself there, singing with the others of the joy of resting, would have seemed incongruous, even absurd. This celebration was for those whose entire life is filled with prayer; it was the culmination of a week spent remembering the divine presence in even the smallest daily acts. It had been a long time since I'd given up this discipline. "God" is a word that still occupies my thoughts but one that I can't connect with anymore.

❄

Detective Nathan Ben-Ami did not look at the man facing him. When Daniel had entered the office, Ben-Ami had shaken his hand and pointed to the tattered leather armchair facing him. He then offered Daniel a cup of coffee, which was refused with a wave of his hand.

Even as he spoke to Daniel, the detective was casting distracted glances at his computer screen. He moved several files, lifting them up and piling them on a low table next to his desk. He took his BlackBerry from his jacket's inside pocket and scrolled down to check his messages. Then he returned to his files, took a sip of coffee, grimaced and turned his head back to his computer, blinking his eyes as he did so.

He still hadn't looked at Daniel. What good would it do? He looked like all the others. Those who'd just been robbed, who'd wrecked their cars or toppled a cyclist. They all had the same worried expression, the same haggard face, the same intense desire: that everything should be put back in order as soon as possible. That he, Detective Ben-Ami – as if he had the power – respond to all the questions bombarding them and then have them sign a few papers so that they could return to the peace of their everyday lives.

Daniel observed the man restlessly moving about in front of him. Rotating in his chair like a weathervane, one eye on a pile of paper and the other on his telephone, Detective Ben-Ami seemed to have little interest in Daniel's presence. His head, enormous in comparison to his small, chubby body and miniscule hands, gave him the appearance of a stray tyrannosaurus, an effect accentuated by his pointy teeth and protruding eyes.

Daniel answered all his questions: when was the last time he had spoken to Sara? Had she been planning a trip? Who did she know in Israel? What did he know about her friends or the company she kept? The questions poured out, one leading into the next, overlapping, as if the police officer already knew all the answers.

After a few minutes of this, Detective Ben-Ami stood and came to sit near Daniel. Elbows planted on his knees, his voluminous head resting on his fists, he looked fixedly at Daniel. "Do you think Sara had any enemies?"

Shocked, Daniel stared back at Ben-Ami. "Enemies? Just what, exactly, are you trying to say?"

"In her entourage, might there be someone jealous of her, someone who might want to harm her?"

"No, why? At least, she didn't tell me anything like that… really, no, I don't get it. She told me about her classmates. She seemed to get along well with them… And no, she's not the type to get involved with drugs, if that's what you're getting at."

The detective pushed his chair back and crossed his legs. He slung his arm over the back of his chair in an attempt to appear relaxed. With an insinuating tone, as if he suspected Daniel of lying, he continued, "What about the romantic side? Did Sara have a boyfriend?"

"She was going out with a guy named Avner for a while, but they broke up a few months ago."

"Why?"

"I'm not sure... it didn't work out, that's all she said."

The detective took a notebook out of his pocket and jotted down a few notes. "And since then?"

"Since what?"

"Uh, well, did she have a relationship... someone in her life?"

"No, I don't think so."

Ben-Ami raised his head, frowned, then looked back down at his notebook and began nervously turning its pages. He watched Daniel from the corner of his eye. "Does the name Ibrahim Awad mean anything to you?"

"No, should it?"

"He was seen with Sara shortly before she disappeared."

"Who... who is he?"

"It seems that he and Sara are very close. Several of her friends mentioned his name. His family hasn't heard from him either. We're trying to find out more."

Daniel's face, which until then had masked his anguish, suddenly froze, revealing that behind the bewilderment was an undeniable fear. His formerly placid voice now gave rise to an imperious and hostile accusation. "But... just exactly what *do* you know? Even so, it's... Someone must have seen Sara... You don't just disappear like that, from one day to the next?"

"Listen, Mr. Benzaken, we're doing everything in our power to find your daughter. We've questioned her professors, her friends, her classmates, everyone who knows her. We checked the contents of her computer and retraced all the calls from her cell phone and at this very moment, an all-points bulletin is circulating in every police station in the country. For now, there's no point wasting energy on speculations."

The telephone rang. Detective Ben-Ami turned back to his desk to answer it. Daniel caught a glimpse of a schoolyard through the open window behind the police officer. The cries of the children at recess rose up in a melodious brouhaha, like the languorous thrum of instruments being tuned before a concert. Daniel again gave in to fatigue – it took no more than a moment of distraction – and voilà, the memories came flooding back, submerging him, carrying him away on their capricious tides. The bell has just rung; he is waiting for Sara outside the schoolyard. She doesn't run to him or jump into his arms, not in front of her schoolmates. But once seated in the back seat of the car, she raises her face to him and, placing a coquettish index finger on her cheek, she demands a kiss. It is the beginning of summer vacation and Daniel is transported back to Saint Adolphe d'Howard and the shores of Lac Vingt-Sous where, a few metres from their chalet, he and Leila had planted a lilac to celebrate Sara's birth. Then suddenly, another memory: back in Montreal, Sara is sitting under the porch of their house on Édouard-Montpetit. She invites Daniel to join her and, with a bunch of lilacs in her hand, she shows him how to detach the flowers to suck out their nectar.

But his impatient spirit prevented him from savouring the scene. Quickly, another image emerged from an even more distant past: close-up on baby Sara. In her bath, she laughs and splashes Daniel. In response to each provocation, he invents a new name for her that she repeats without understanding, and he splashes her with renewed vigour: Saradio, Saravenous, Saratatouille, Saravioli, Saravishing... Daniel pulled himself together. No, he had to stop this immediately. The slippery slope of memories was too dangerous. Especially now.

The detective finished his phone call. He got up and stepped toward Daniel with his hand extended. "Trust me, we're doing everything we can to find your daughter," he repeated. "And obviously, if you hear anything..." Daniel let himself be guided out, thanked the policeman and went down the long corridor leading to the exit. The office door that closed behind him, the receptionist who gave him a compassionate look, the taxi driver who insisted on putting his

suitcase in the trunk himself: it all seemed like a conspiracy to remind him that his life was now in suspense. He appeared to others,
and even to himself, as no more than that: a man whose daughter
has disappeared, a man who is worried, a man who waits.

❈

"I hope nothing has happened to her." This little sentence to
which his conscience was moored covered a labyrinth of questions
and concerns: Maybe Sara was attacked... or she had an accident
and was injured... But Daniel refused to put words to his fear.
Superstitiously, perhaps, to resist the anxiety that threatened him, all
these images are quickly neutralized by that insignificant little sentence: "I hope nothing has happened to her."

❈

Jerusalem. October 16, 2008
I share my room with a student named Samira. She talks a lot.
Especially about herself, her family members, who still live in
Jerusalem, her law studies – "What a bore!" she says – and her
passion for poetry. She glances at the little shelf above her bed and
then jumps up to get a book in English, the works of Keats. She
opens it, almost randomly (though in fact it's a poem she practically
knows by heart, "La Belle Dame sans Merci," and starts to read,
punctuating each verse with theatrical movements of her hands. "He
died when he was only 25," she explains, "But his ideas are those of
an old man!" Her enthusiasm seems a bit forced. It's as if all these
words, all these grand gestures that seem to imitate an imaginary
avalanche, are there to create a diversion, as if there's a knot of
sadness inside her that cannot be revealed.
Samira told me that it was her father who had encouraged her
to study law. She isn't unhappy but she's tempted to call it quits.
"I'm tired of cramming my brain with all these articles of law, all

these clauses and corollaries. There are more important things in life. My parents don't understand any of this. They want my future to be assured. They tell me I shouldn't have to depend on anyone. And basically, they're right. But what good are these studies, what good is a career if I stay empty inside? All this work means nothing if you don't aspire to something more: the desire to learn, to enrich your life with new ideas, to discover other resources within yourself. That counts, too, don't you think?" Samira looks imploringly at me, as if I were the one forcing her to become a lawyer. "The other day," she continued, "I gave my father a book of poems by Mahmoud Darwish. He hardly looked at it, then he politely thanked me, as if I'd handed him a cheap tie. When I mentioned it again the next Friday, you know what he said? 'Poetry is for dreamers, and dreamers never did anything to change the world. Pretty words won't save us from oppression.' I didn't say a word. I know full well poetry won't bring us peace. But if we don't have words, if we don't have stories – well, what do you think about that?"

Samira wanted my support. I could see it in her expectant look and the fervour in her eyes – she looked like the professor who can scarcely keep himself from whispering the correct answer to his student. I know what I should have said. I should have said that resistance is communicated through the story, that it's everyone's duty to tell it, that true solidarity is not just being scandalized by violence and the world's indifference – it's being committed, witnessing, writing – right now – the story that will be our future. But I have never been seduced by that kind of idealism. And besides, how could I discuss such a topic with Samira without revealing that I'm not only Muslim but also, and equally, Jewish? That I also bear within me my father's memories, the stories about the war, which he himself did not experience, but which had permeated his consciousness nonetheless?

So I chose to say nothing. And to show her that she could see in me, if not an ally, then at least a benevolent friend, I asked her to loan me the book of Keats' poetry that she still held in her hand.

From: Sara
To: Daniel
Subject: Jerusalem
Friday, October 17, 2008, 2:20 p.m.

Hi Papa!

I hope you're well. I have so many things to tell you. First, I finally met my research director, Shlomo Oren. A bit cold at first, but he gets excited when he talks about his work. He supervises the excavations at Khirbet Qeiyafa, an archaeological dig southwest of Jerusalem. Apparently that's where David slew Goliath. He convinced me to join his group. We leave in early November.

I've met a lot of foreign students at the university: Australians, French, Germans. About ten of us are taking the biblical archaeology seminar and we all go for a drink together in the evening. My roommate's name is Samira. Very passionate – about poetry, movies... and boys! She's registered in the law program (to please her father) but she dreams about writing. We get along well, even if I do sometimes find her irritating.

That's it for now. I can't wait to talk to you.

Sara

From: Daniel
To: Sara
Subject: News from Montreal
Friday, October 17, 2008, 10:53 p.m.

Dear Sara,

Thank you for the latest news. I miss you. Fortunately, I have my classes to prepare and that keeps me busy. I'm teaching a course on Flemish painting this fall. Last week we studied Rembrandt's biblical paintings. On that note, do you know where the saying "the writing is on the wall" comes from? It's actually an allusion to the same Bible story that inspired Belshazzar's Feast. A divine hand appears to King Belshazzar and writes on the wall the decree that announces the end of his empire. I've taught this painting for twenty years, but it was only today that one of my students helped me see the connection.

I'll be in the country tomorrow. Call me Sunday instead.

Big hug,

Your father who loves you

❄

Once back in his hotel room, Daniel drew the curtains. He sat on the edge of the bed, took his phone out of his jacket's inside pocket and dialled Sara's number. He had performed this ritual for the past week, a gesture faithfully repeated every hour, every day. It was the act that, despite its banal appearance, still managed to convince him that nothing had changed, that everything would soon fall into place.

He called: no answer. Surely there was an explanation. On a whim, she'd gone off on a desert excursion with friends. She might have lost her phone or forgotten the charger. She might even have fallen madly in love, holed up with a boy for a week and simply decided to escape from the world. Perhaps… Drained, Daniel collapsed on the bed.

He woke up with a start. His heart was beating hard. It was anxiety, a ravine opening up within him. How long had he slept? How could he sleep while – but he was exhausted, and sleep was no longer a pleasure.

Daniel closed his eyes again. Where did that memory come from? How did it slip into the present? It was a fall weekend 15 years ago, and he and Sara were walking on Mount Royal. The first

21

snow had fallen but had melted almost immediately. Sara stopped on the side of the path. Daniel approached and saw the dead bird.

Daniel takes Sara's hand, trying to lead her away, but she refuses to leave. "We have to take care of him." She speaks in such a tone that there is no contradicting her. On her knees at the base of a tree, she begins to dig with a branch that she finds on the ground. But the earth is too hard and the branch breaks. "I need a shovel." Standing by helplessly, Daniel surveys the area. Where is he going to find a shovel? He reluctantly takes a dozen steps toward the lake and collects a few bits of wood. When he returns, Sara does not turn around. She has found a sharp stone and is using it to strike the ground with all her might. Despite her valiant efforts, she has made only a small depression in the earth. At this pace, they'll be there all afternoon. Resigned, Daniel gets down on his knees and, with a movement whose impatience he instantly regrets, takes the stone from her hands. He sweats and swears and skins his knuckles but soon manages to hollow out an opening just big enough to receive the bird. Meanwhile, Sara uses the elastic from her hair to bind together the twigs they have gathered. "It's a fan," she explains, "to chase away bad spirits." She sends him off to find more twigs for the feet and pine cones for the eyes. He returns. "No, those are too big." He goes again to find smaller ones. He is cold and tired and poorly hides his bad mood, but yet he is already angry at himself for not playing the game with more enthusiasm.

He should have gone along with Sara, taken her more seriously, even pre-empted her: "Why not decorate the fan with ribbons? What if we carve the bird's name on a stone to put on the mound?" But Daniel is only thinking of getting back home; he's afraid of getting a sore throat. After all, the next day he is scheduled to meet a gallery director who is interested in his recent paintings, and he sincerely hopes to make a good impression.

Remembering this episode, Daniel regretted not having been in the moment, as if he had been no more than a helpless witness, a stranger to the urgent enterprise into which Sara had tried to lead him. Stretched out on the bed in his hotel room, he contemplated the scene that passed slowly before his eyes, watching for new details that might once have gone unnoticed. And the haunting pain that he allowed to flow through him came not only from this lost moment in time but also from the realization that this past had never really belonged to him. This double absence – that of the memory and then his own as an exile from the memory – made the uneasiness that gnawed at him even harder to bear.

❄

Jerusalem, October 19, 2008
I talked to Papa on the phone tonight. He asked a lot of questions. He wanted reassurance, to make sure that I'm eating well, that I have friends and that my classes are interesting. I wasn't very enthusiastic, but I tried to dispel his anxiety. I described my days in infinite detail: my meals, what I'm reading, who I see. I quickly realized he wasn't very interested. What he really wanted was to talk about the past, about Mama and the vacations we'd taken together. "The other day, I was looking for my passport and I came upon a picture of you holding a horseshoe crab by the tail. I think it was in Maine, or maybe Cape Cod. You were wearing a dark-blue bathing suit. You must have been 12 or 13. Do you remember?" He didn't give me a chance to answer before continuing. "The beach was strewn with those crabs, there were so many you had to watch where you stepped to avoid crushing them. That morning, we met an old man walking on the beach with his dog. He explained to you that these bizarre creatures, which look like a soldier's helmet, are among the oldest in the world and that they haven't changed in almost 500 million years. He also said that they come onto the sand to mate but that some end up roasting in the sun and by the end of the day, half of them will be dead. When the man left, you started picking the crabs up by the tail and throwing them as far as you could into the sea. You'd run toward the waves, a horseshoe crab in each hand, yelling, 'We can't let them die!' Do you remember?"

From his voice, I could tell that Papa was feeling emotional. He was talking about horseshoe crabs, but he was thinking about Mama, sitting under her beach umbrella with her feet buried in the sand. I hesitantly replied that I did remember that day, the photo and my dark-blue bathing suit, but he wasn't fooled. But he so needed me to remember. It was as if without me, the memory might vanish, as if he needed the weight of our two mental images to preserve it and if one of us gave up, the other would also lose his grip, allowing the memory to disappear like a balloon carried off by the wind. Even when I hung up, I felt that he was still waiting for some comforting words, an assurance, perhaps, that he wasn't all alone in his past. So I blamed myself for not having been a better liar.

Jerusalem, October 19, 2008, 2 a.m.
Papa, I should have understood you better, I should have known how to respond. But honestly, I really wracked my brain – I just don't have the same memories as you. The only thing I remember is those gargoyles you sculpted in the sand. They looked like Gothic monsters rising from the depths of the earth. You made them with great gaping mouths and sent me to look for bits of white shell to use for their teeth. And – I never told you this – I had nightmares about them that night.

I also remember that shortly after one of those summers we spent in New England, Mama was hospitalized for the first time. I remember your pain and everything you never wanted to talk about afterwards, even several years after she died. You shut yourself into the bathroom so that I wouldn't see you cry. The doctors had implied that there was no chance of remission, but you always made me believe that she would survive. And when I went back to school, you smiled, even though there was nothing but fear in your eyes.

You never wanted to recall those long, anguished months of waiting, those nights you didn't sleep because Mama had spent the day vomiting and the nights when we breathed a little easier because the test results had been a bit better. What did you and Mama talk

*about when you sat by her bed and held her hand, waiting for the
doctor to come? What were you thinking about as you paced the
hospital corridor, the day of her last operation? You didn't pray, you
didn't know how to, so how did you occupy your mind? Were you
perhaps remembering the first moments you and Mama spent
together? Your walks on Mount Royal or along the Lachine Canal?
Or maybe you dreamed of the trips that we would take together and
the cities we would visit if only the doctors had been wrong, if against
all expectations, Mama would get well. The nurse sent you home that
day. She had seen the dark circles under your eyes, your drawn face,
your slightly staggering gait and she convinced you that you needed to
rest. She promised to call as soon as the operation was over.*

*Since you couldn't sit still, I suggested a game of checkers. At first,
you tried to concentrate. You followed the game, eyebrows knit, and
you took the time to think before each move. Then your attention
flagged and you began to lose. I chewed up your checkers, two, three,
four at a time. I told myself that those victories were a sign. If I won
every round, it meant the operation would be a success and Mama
would leave the hospital and come home cured. Your successive
defeats didn't seem to bother you; you were resigned, as if I really was
too strong for you. Maybe also, knowing my superstitions, you decided
to let me win, seeking in my childish hope a refuge to calm your own
distress.*

*When the telephone finally rang, at about 8 p.m., you jumped
up to answer. You held the receiver tightly against your ear, as if you
didn't want me to hear the doctor's voice. I saw you grow pale and I
saw your face fall apart, like a drawing in the sand that the tide s
lowly erases. The words I had so dreaded, that I had said over and
over again in my prayers to imprison them, to assure myself that they
would never see the light of day, those words that would open an abyss
within me every time I let my thoughts approach "Mama is dead" –
those words you did not say. You looked at me and, certain that I had
understood, simply repeated what the doctor had said: "It was too
much for her heart."*

※

Detective Ben-Ami finally called back. Daniel had been leaving him message after message for three full days. "Sorry, Mr. Benzaken, nothing new for now. We'll keep you posted." The detective is more courteous and even more amiable the less he has to tell, Daniel said to himself.

So Daniel insisted: "But, still, you must have an idea. Is it… is it possible she was kidnapped? Maybe… if she's had an accident… Surely someone must have seen her…"

There was a long silence at the other end of the line. Not wanting to leave himself open to criticism, the detective interrupted Daniel. "Mr. Benzaken," he finally said in a weary voice, "Believe me when I say that I understand your concern, but we can't rule out any hypothesis at this time. Our entire network has been put on alert. Sara's picture is making the rounds of every police station in the nation. As soon as we hear anything, we'll let you know."

※

Daniel had been in Jerusalem a full week but was still living on Montreal time. Awake since dawn, he was the only customer in the hotel's restaurant. He ate without appetite or pleasure and thus without guilt. He ate because it was necessary, because Sara needed him. His thoughts went no further than that. "Something has happened to Sara." He must not add flesh to the bones of these words. On second thought, was it possible that nothing serious had happened? A simple misunderstanding. She thought she had told him that she was going on a trip, or she had lost her phone, and that was all.

The dream that had so violently awakened him was still on his mind. Leila's presence in particular continued to envelop him, like a fairy-tale creature, simultaneously desired and feared, who lingers in a child's bedroom after the book is closed and the light turned off.

Daniel went back over his dream. He is in Detective Ben-Ami's office. Ben-Ami moves the files piled up on his desk. He finally sits down and gives Daniel a severe, solemn look:

"I regret to inform you that your daughter has been arrested."

"What does that mean? What has she done?"

"Unfortunately, I am not authorized to tell you that. It could compromise the investigation. Just be aware that... if she is found guilty, she could go to prison."

"I don't understand. There must be a misunderstanding."

"Useless to speculate, Mr. Benzaken. Sara must appear before the judge tomorrow. As soon as we know more, we will tell you, of course."

And the detective walks him to the door, patting his back in a friendly manner. Leila is waiting for him in the hallway. She wears a dark suit, a hat and black gloves. Daniel thinks: a woman in mourning. Leila takes his hand and covers it with her gloved fingers, the white oyster a willing prisoner in a black shell. She gives him the affectionate smile she had given him in the early days, the smile she had offered when he came to join her in the evening in the months after they had first met. Yet Daniel is certain that he can read something more than tenderness in her gaze. She remains silent, but it's as if she has already said it all: "Why didn't you put up a fight? That detective doesn't have the right to hide the truth from us. We have to know, Daniel, we have to do everything we can for our daughter."

In the hotel dining room, Daniel forced himself to drink a glass of orange juice as he mentally reviewed the dream's scenario. Since Sara's disappearance, the memory of Leila was often with him, like a benevolent apparition. It was a presence without colour or texture, only the certainty that a being was there, watching him, guessing his thoughts, moulding itself to his movements. In the silence, she held him back and prevented him from completely disappearing into himself – like Sara who, on Sunday mornings, used to tiptoe into the studio where Daniel was painting, and from her perch on a stool, would watch each one of his movements, anchoring her eyes to each stroke of the brush.

Now Leila even intruded on his dreams. She too wanted answers. Now the two of them bore the weight of concern and in their shared anguish, Daniel rediscovered the nervous intimacy of their first years when, bent over Sara's cradle, they waited for a fever to drop. In the darkness that slowly enveloped him, Daniel no longer felt so alone, even though the voice wending its way toward him was only a creature in his mind's eye.

※

Jerusalem, October 20, 2008
In his book Jerusalem: Battlegrounds of Memory, *writer Amos Elon describes Jerusalem as "the city with three sabbaths": Friday for the Muslims, Saturday for the Jews and Sunday for the Christians. I love the idea of a four-day week!*

Jerusalem, October 21, 2008
Not long after Mama died, Papa started talking to me about her. At first, our only concern was to keep going, to keep ourselves from falling into the abyss that had opened up in front of us. I remember my first thought, waking up in the morning, was always, "I have to hold on until tonight." I assigned myself tasks and put all my energy into completing them: today, I have to clean my room, do the shopping on my way home from school, answer condolence letters. The future, where I had put all my dreams, was closed to me. There was nothing but the pitiful present: the meal to make for Papa and myself, lessons to learn and homework to finish.

The contradictory and violent feelings that tumbled about within me – how could I share them with Papa without being afraid that I'd make him stumble and fall? How could I tell him about the fear that engulfed me just as I fell asleep, because I feared Mama's fleeting presence in my dreams and its even more agonizing disappearance when I awoke? How could I admit to him that every morning as I waited on the subway platform, I said to myself, "Well then, if I wanted to, I could end this all right now, painlessly and without any effort at all?" The result: Papa and I spoke very little. We were too lost and adrift to feel a bond. There are tragedies that bring people together, but Mama's death pulled us apart.

Several years had to pass before we could begin to share our memories. We'd walk by a candy store, for example, and he'd say, "Look, Carambars! Remember how your mother loved Carambars?" And to please him, I suggested that we buy some and then pretended that I liked them, too. I took advantage of those moments to ask him questions, to find out what the two of them had been like before I was born.

That's how Papa ended up telling me about how they first met. He was finishing his doctorate in art history; the long hours spent reading meant he was sacrificing sleep. His left eye had become inflamed and at about 1 a.m. one winter night, he made his way to a pharmacy on Côte-des-Neiges in search of a remedy. He scarcely noticed the raven-haired young woman behind the counter. When she brought her face close to his to look at his eye, he failed to notice that she was smiling at him. And when she explained that it was nothing serious, just a minor irritation, he listened with half an ear. He was thinking only of paying for the bottle of drops that she'd given him and getting home to finish his chapter.

It wasn't until a few weeks later, after he had submitted his thesis, that the memory of the young pharmacist resurfaced. "Suddenly," explained Papa, "I remembered that her eyes were green and that she was wearing a vanilla perfume. All kinds of details came back to me. I remembered her long, thin fingers and her nostrils that flared slightly when she examined my eye. I don't know if it was because I was relieved to have finished my doctorate or because I didn't know what to focus on after those longs months of work, but I began to think about her every day. It was sort of like retroactively falling in love at first sight, a delayed-reaction romance. Of course, it was all *absurd. In my flashes of lucidity, I told myself that she probably didn't even remember me. But the image of her face, amplified by my idle thoughts, kept coming back to me."*

So he went back to the pharmacy. This time, she was busy with another client. How would he approach her? What might he say? "Hi, do you remember me?" She might smile at him, but then what? He certainly couldn't invite her for a glass of wine, out of the blue like that. So without really thinking about what he was doing, he began to vigorously rub his left eye until it became red. Then he approached the counter where the young woman was standing. She recognized him immediately. "It doesn't look like it's gotten much better." This time he noticed her smile, which bore a hint of irony. "You know, you should stop rubbing your eye like that, you're only making things worse." Papa didn't know how to respond. All his life, he explained, he had never been able to make the first move. So he left again with another bottle of drops, cursing himself for not being more courageous.

He continued this little game for a few days, taking special care to rub his eye before entering the pharmacy but never realizing that the black-haired woman had not been fooled. In the end, she was the one who took the lead: "You know, you don't have to hurt your eye like that. If you're free tonight, why not ask me to join you for a glass of wine instead?"

Jerusalem, October 22, 2008
When Mama got sick, prayer became my sanctuary. At first, I prayed to have "all the odds go in my favour." Each blessing added weight, tipping the scale toward the chance that my mother would live. I recited the verses from the Koran that I knew, the ones Mama herself said every morning. I had said them so often that they could have rapidly and effortlessly strung themselves together without my help, but I denied myself all mechanical practices. Not only was it imperative that every word be spoken sincerely, but it had to be fully imbued with its meaning. Each word was a hand held out toward

God, each invocation of His name, a call that kept Him present. And if I was distracted, even once, by a bird that came to sit on my window sill or by Papa's alarm clock, I had to start all over again. Then there were prayers in Hebrew. Standing with my feet together, I recited the 18 blessings. I repeated the eighth several times: "Blessed art thou, o Lord, our God, King of the universe, He who heals the sick."

But He didn't listen to me. All those hours when I felt His living presence within me were nothing but lost moments in time. I remained alone, imprisoned in words that never escaped from my heart.

ABRAHAM LIVED A LONG LIFE, each day the voice of God opening his mind's eye a bit more.

After years of plenitude, however, questions cleared a path through him.

The presence of His words no longer sufficed. Abraham demanded a sign.

He had smashed the stone idols, those false representations of the great beyond where man's desires took refuge.

That which he saw, he shared with his brethren.

"God is not where you seek to find Him. God is not that *thing*, and that thing, no matter how beautiful or whole or noble it may be, will never bring you closer to Him. Forget these solid forms. Close your eyes. Let the words, which are not the words of man, come to you."

Abraham had lived with the whisper of God joined to his steps.

Yet doubt continued to burrow through his veins.

Did this call, which had torn him from his people, not come from within himself, after all? This voice, intended for him, was it not the voice of the man called Abraham?

"What could this God be, this source of all I see, if I am His creator?"

Once born into his heart, the anguish never leaves him.

Sarah's smile, which once drew him back to the world and restored his confidence, only irritates him, a gesture of kindness to which he alone knows he has no right.

Abraham goes away, walking for three days and three nights, scarcely stopping to rest.

Alone, he takes refuge on Mount Moriah. High on the mountain, the mist, heavy with odours of the earth, brings him back to himself for a moment.

2

Rooted in place, Daniel could not take his eyes off of the hand of
Professor Oren, who invited him to sit down across from him. He
contemplated his long bony fingers, the bitten nails, the energetic
wrist whose protruding veins formed, with surprising clarity, the letter *aleph*, the first letter of the Hebrew alphabet. Daniel stared at
the professor's hand because he was afraid to meet his eyes. The
compassion that appeared on everyone's face – an empathy both
curious and detached – was something that Daniel had learned to
recognize during the week he'd been in Israel. It was unbearable.

Shlomo Oren's smile, however, displayed sincere warmth.

"I don't know what to tell you, Mr. Benzaken... I don't understand. I don't think Sara's the type to leave without letting someone
know."

"No, she's not."

"I assume you've spoken with the police detective. What did he
tell you?"

"Not much. He opened an investigation, but for the moment,
they have no clues. At least that's what I was led to believe."

"As you probably know, Sara and I meet every Tuesday. This was
the first time she missed a meeting."

"Yes... do you know if there was... if there was a change that
could explain?"

"Not really. Sara is pretty discreet... but she has a number of
friends, she isn't all alone here. Lately, I've been seeing her quite
often with a Palestinian student. A big guy with a beard, a bit of a
dreamer."

"Yes, I know about that. According to the police, he seems to
have disappeared as well."

Professor Oren seemed surprised. "Oh, really? So maybe they're together."

"It's possible. Do you know this student?"

"Yes, a little. His name is Ibrahim. Ibrahim Awad. He's taken only one class with me. An odd character, always has his nose in a book. He speaks perfect Hebrew and can recite entire chapters of the Bible and the Koran... At the end of the last session, he turned in a strange but fascinating essay where he tried to show that the biblical character of Abraham was tortured by doubt and that the famous sacrifice of Isaac was nothing but a challenge aimed at God to summon Him and demand proof of His existence?"

"Sara never talked about him."

"Really? But ever since they met, they've been practically inseparable."

"Before Ibrahim, Sara was with someone named Avner. Do you know him?"

"I saw them together a few times... He came to meet her after class from time to time. He owns a restaurant. Several restaurants, in fact. Maybe you should speak to Sara's roommate. They're very close. There's also Tamar, another one of my students. She and Sara worked together on the dig during our last trip to Khirbet Qeiyafa."

Daniel looked up at Professor Oren, who gazed back at him with a detached look. His sense of decency kept him from letting on that he recognized Daniel's distress.

❊

Jerusalem, October 24, 2008
Conversation overheard in a café. Five or six British tourists, sitting at the bar behind me. One of them asked, "And you, what do you do?" A man's voice answered, "I do a little bit of everything and a lot of nothing." I wanted to turn around to see his face but I didn't dare.

Jerusalem, October 25, 2008

This morning, I got up very early. It must have been 5 a.m. since it was still dark. I got dressed quickly and walked toward the Arab Quarter. My footsteps resonated in the narrow alleys at the end of which I could see busy shadows, a man bent over from the load of sacks full of spices and dried fruits he carried on his back, two women in quiet conversation in the entryway to a house. I walked to the Damascus Gate, then retraced my steps. The sun was just coming up and a few merchants had already opened their shops.

At the curve of a lane, near El-Wad Street, I stopped to look at the backgammon games in a little boutique that sold all kinds of wooden objects. Boxes of all sizes, salad bowls, goblets, fountain pens, cup-and-ball games: the shelves were bursting with trinkets and trifles, some more useful than others, all emitting the penetrating odour of resin. A friendly-looking man approached me. In broken English, he asked me if I was interested in the backgammon game. He assumed I was a tourist. More in an effort to correct his error than because I wanted to buy the game, I answered him in Arabic. "How much is this one?" His features suddenly relaxed, as if he'd just recognized a familiar voice, and he asked me where I was from. I explained that my mother was Lebanese, that I was born in Montreal and that I had come to Jerusalem to study. The conversation got underway and he asked me several questions about Canada, life in North America and about the Palestinians I knew there. His curiosity seemed so natural, so free of any ulterior motive, that I went ahead and told him about my studies, my doubts, and my plans for the future. And seeing that I hadn't hesitated to open up to him, he told me his story.

After the Nakba in 1948, his father's three brothers, all shopkeepers in Jerusalem, took refuge in Jordan. Only his father stayed behind, despite the threats and the violence. Thanks to his perseverance, he managed to save the house, which was a few streets away from the shop. The man explained that he had been only 10 at the time of the Nakba, but he still remembered nights spent in the cellar, huddled next to his brothers under a damp blanket, waiting for the fighting to stop. His mother had died giving birth to his little sister a few years later, and his father had raised them alone. He then questioned me about my mother and her family and their life in Lebanon. There was a curiosity in his eyes that seemed full of kindness. As if refusing to see me as a simple stranger, he held onto even the smallest details that could connect us: language, history, exile. I told him about Mama's past, how she had left Lebanon during the civil war, her life in Paris with her parents and brother, her pharmacy studies and how she had met my father.

"And your father, is he Lebanese too?" the man asked.

"No, Moroccan." And after a slight hesitation, I added, "A Moroccan Jew." I used the Jewish word yehudi as if to correct my first statement, as if it had been inaccurate to simply say he was Moroccan. When I saw his reaction, I was instantly angry at myself. His expression, which had been so warm just a few minutes earlier, turned to ice; his features hardened as if he had been wearing a mask that, after being animated for a moment, had returned to its habitual rigidity.

But I shouldn't have been angry at myself. After all, I'd only been trying to be honest. How is it that some people feel betrayed at the very moment they hear the truth? If I'd told him about my double attachment right off the bat, would he have understood me better?

There are some words that, once said, take you far beyond what you want them to mean. "Yehudi." Telling this man that my father was Jewish was all it took to put a wall up between us. That word alone meant, "We are strangers. I don't want to know about your life, and you will not know about mine." His silence was full of bitterness: "You and your people, you feel nothing but hatred for us. You speak Arabic, you pretend to be interested in my situation, but you're just like all the others: a hypocrite trying to ease her conscience."

I looked at him for a long moment, seeking the smallest opening in the closed expression on his face, a tiny trace of what had, for a brief moment, brought us together. But the mask remained *impenetrable, so I thanked him and left. As I picked my way through the maze of Jerusalem's streets, I wondered which of the two of us had been the least faithful to himself: me, who regretted having told him my father was Jewish, or the man, who had unwittingly opened himself up to "an enemy of his people."*

Jerusalem, October 26, 2008
When did things get so complicated? When I was little, I didn't need to know what it meant to be Jewish or Muslim. With Mama, I woke at dawn and joined her in her prayers. With Papa, I read the Bible stories: Abraham and the birth of Isaac, David and Jonathan, Joseph's betrayal by his brothers, Deborah, Esther... I asked nothing more. My days organized themselves quite naturally around these rituals, the Salat al-Subh *in the morning and the* Shema *(the only prayer Papa knew by heart) in the evening. For me, there was no separation between Arabic and Hebrew, between the sumptuous* iftars *to which we invited Mama's cousins and the Passover meals that Papa's mother prepared when we visited her in Vancouver. I didn't try to imagine what God might be like or question His existence. I was content to repeat the gestures Mama had taught me and, in my prayers, He was present.*

My life as a child was dominated by my needs, so for God, I had only requests. The praises didn't have much power over me. I didn't understand their purpose. I told myself that if God is almighty, he is self-sufficient – what use does He have for man's admiration or submission? On the other hand, I found a thousand reasons to ask for his help and support. I asked for myself and my family and friends of course, but also on behalf of others. At the time, I had developed the habit of watching the evening news with Papa. Sarajevo, Chechnya, Rwanda, all those names of faraway places summed up hate, violence and my impotence as I faced the misery unfolding before my eyes. Prayer was only a refuge. It served to convince me that, secretly, I could act: a way to refuse indifference. The most minor events had become a pretext for prayer. This applied not only to the air disasters,

hostage-takings and earthquakes that captured my attention. An
ambulance siren was enough to make me close my eyes and whisper,
"Dear God, I beg you, heal the sick, help the injured, gather the souls
of the dead."

Now all those prayers remain silent within me. I still tell myself
that I am Jewish, that I am Muslim, but in practice, it doesn't really
mean much anymore.

✳

From: Daniel
To: Sara
Subject: News
Monday, October 27, 2008, 7:24 a.m.

Dear Sara,

I was so happy to talk to you yesterday. After our conversation, I
went to get a few logs from the basement and made a fire in the
fireplace.

The apartment is so empty without you.

I forgot to tell you: last Thursday as I was coming out of the library,
I ran into Stéphane Bensoussan. Remember him? There was a time
when his parents often invited you to Friday night dinner. I guess it's
been a while since you've seen each other. He asked a lot of questions about you, but don't worry, I was very discreet. He told me
he's in his third year of dental school. It's funny, I imagined him
more in philosophy or literature.

In the U.S., the election campaign is in full swing. A few of my colleagues seem to have caught the fever. They speculate that Obama
will win and that there'll be an American renaissance. You know me
– these dreams of change always leave me a bit skeptical.

All my love,

Papa

Shlomo Oren couldn't say for certain, but he thought that Avner's restaurant was called Delights of Djerba. "In any case, I'm pretty sure there's a 'Djerba' in there," he told Daniel. At the hotel, Daniel learned that there was indeed a restaurant called The Djerba Palace in the Nahalat Shiva neighbourhood. He quickly hailed a taxi.

The restaurant's terrace was empty. Once inside, his eyes were slow to adjust to the darkness. The same thing happened to him in Montreal, when his eyes were half-blinded by the whiteness of the snow. A young woman appeared – all smiles and a plunging neckline – and invited him to sit down. He was the only customer. Little by little, the details of the décor came into focus: on the walls, a sunny fresco – white roofs and blue sky – borrowed from a tourist magazine on the Mediterranean; from the ceiling, painted like the starry heavens, hung multicoloured paper lanterns like the ones found in Chinese restaurants; on the floor lay old red-and-blue carpets vaguely evocative of Turkey or Iran; in the back, near the bathrooms, sat a burgundy velvet ottoman, the sort one might find in a 19th-century French salon. In sum, the person who had arranged this cache of objects had probably never set foot on the island of Djerba.

The waitress returned to his table. This time Daniel noticed her eyes, their burning curiosity smothered by two sleepy eyelids.

"Do you know what you'd like to have?" The languor, the slow drawl of her voice reminded Daniel of a 1950s movie star.

"A cocoa, please. Tell me, do you know if the owner… if Avner… is here?"

The young woman gave Daniel a severe look. Her curiosity had turned into suspicion.

"Do you know him?"

"Actually, yes. No, not really… Let's just say… he knows my daughter."

"I'll see if he's here."

A few minutes later, the waitress came back. With an abrupt movement, looking outside toward the terrace, she put his cocoa on the table.

"He'll be here later."

"That's fine. I'll wait." He took his phone out of his pocket again. It was the labour of hope, superstition, the suffering of immobility that drove him to call, and to continue to call, every 10 minutes. As long as he could obstinately, blindly and absurdly dial her number, Sara remained attached to him and he could keep her presence near.

Slowly, the restaurant's terrace filled up. A young couple, sitting in the shade of a parasol, smiled as they watched a baby boy wailing at the next table. The mother – a woman with long curly hair, make-up and a manicure – looked back at the couple, a false look of distress arching her brows. Turning her back to the stroller, she apologized for her child's howling as she distractedly shook a rattle in front of his face. The young lovers – a serious-looking boy and a plump, smiling young woman – held their hands out to the woman and reassured her: "Not at all, don't worry, it doesn't bother us, on the contrary…"

Before Sara was born, Leila had never tired of looking at other people's babies either. In parks, in outdoor cafés, she bent over baby carriages, her eyes full of admiration. Normally so timid, she engaged in conversation with the mothers, asked questions and gave advice. Daniel was also drawn in, abandoning his finger to a baby's energetic hand as he babbled compliments.

The two sweethearts on the terrace then stood and walked away, arms around each other. The presumptuous certainty in which they draped themselves, that confidence that overlooked all the details and attached itself only to frozen images, silent and pristine, of the future – marriage, apartment, children – he and Leila had also experienced it. If on one of their walks, Daniel and Leila happened to pass a young mother with her newborn in her arms, they were easily convinced, without having to deliberate, imagine or hypothesize, that one day they too would be parents.

Daniel was startled. He hadn't heard the waitress approaching. The indifference in her gaze was chilling.

"Mr. Elfassi just arrived. He knows you're here."

❊

From: Sara
To: Daniel
Subject: When are you coming to Jerusalem?
Tuesday, October 28, 2008, 11:10 p.m.

Good evening, Papa.
I miss you too.
Yes, I remember Stéphane.
I'm thinking a lot about the past these days. It's as if leaving Montreal and transplanting myself in a foreign country has suddenly made me feel like I have to gather all the pieces of my life together.
I can't wait to see you! Are you coming at the end of December?
Kisses.

❊

Jerusalem, October 27, 2008
"In Jerusalem, and I mean within the ancient walls, I walk from one epoch to another without a memory to guide me. The prophets over there are sharing the history of the holy... ascending to heaven and returning less discouraged and melancholy, because love and peace are holy and are coming to town."
  Mahmoud Darwish

Jerusalem, October 28, 2008
It was during the Second Intifada in 2000 that I began to be aware of the contradictions stirring inside me. As long as it only concerned

*prayers and rituals, things were easier. I adopted a discipline that
nourished my spirit and made sense only to me. I didn't feel the need
to share it with anyone else. But when it came to belonging to a
group – the Jewish or the Muslim community, the Moroccans or the
Lebanese – I felt disoriented.*

*Papa had noticed my curiosity, so he enrolled me in a Hebrew
school, a Talmud Torah where I went every Sunday morning to learn
a few rudiments of Jewish religion and history. Directed by a sour,
shrivelled-up old rabbi, the school had only a dozen students, a
disparate group of kids of all ages who regarded him with boredom
and anxiously awaited the moment when they could finally go join
their friends in the park. The old professor's classes, devoid of any
apparent structure, consisted of making us repeat ad nauseum verses
from the Torah and teaching us lists of vocabulary. He also taught us
the* mitzvot, *and every time one of us asked why we were forbidden to
eat seafood or to turn on the lights on the Sabbath, he would frown
and answer, coming nose to nose with the insolent one, "Because the
Holy One, blessed be He, commanded it – that's why."*

*I had been seated next to a boy my own age, a Moroccan Jew
whose parents had just come to Montreal. His name was Stéphane
Bensoussan, and I believed that I detected in his sad, dark-circled eyes
a longing for Meknes, the city where he'd been born. The rabbi had
put the two of us at the back of the class: me because I was a girl –
the only one in the group – and Stéphane because he asked too many
questions. Since our teacher had decided to ignore us, it was only
natural that we ignore him back, and we spent most of our time
whispering and exchanging caricatures. Stéphane told me about his
school, which he hated, about his parents, of whom he was ashamed,
and about his older sister, with whom he constantly fought.*

*From time to time, he invited me to dinner at his house on
Friday night. I have only vague memories of those Shabbat meals. I
remember only his father's doleful, monotonous voice as he recited the
Kiddush, the blessing over the wine, his mother's melancholy smile as
she insisted I take a second helping of tomato salad, the nasty looks*

that Stéphane and his sister exchanged across the table. I felt as if my presence was the only thing keeping them from skinning each other alive and that I'd been invited only to bring a few minutes of peace into their tumultuous daily life.

After the meal, we all sat in front of the television to watch French variety shows. I knew only Michel Fugain and Joe Dassin, so I was fascinated by these parades of celebrities. I listened, captivated, as these aging stars, their smooth faces fixed in an eternal smile, recounted their battles with alcohol, their victory over depression and their rediscovered happiness. Every so often, Stéphane's mother gently tilted her head toward me to explain that this was so-and-so's third husband or to tell me why another one had refused to speak to his father for 10 years.

As for Stéphane, he looked at all of us in consternation. He would snigger each time one of the celebrities made himself look ridiculous and ended up leading me, somewhat against my will, into his room. There, we talked about Jules Verne, he showed me his telescope, drew the constellations for me and explained how stars were born. I didn't understand all of it although I was touched by his enthusiasm and sincerity. I don't remember if we kissed, but I seem to remember him standing behind me as my eye squinted against the telescope's lens and putting his hand on my shoulder. It seems to me that something happened just then; I just can't picture his face or imagine his mouth approaching mine. Maybe it's only a distant dream after all, taking advantage of my failing memory to try to pass itself off as something I really remember.

And then one day, everything fell apart. It was a Friday evening in late September 2000, at the beginning of what would soon be known as the Second Intifada. Stéphane's sister, Sandrine, asked a question, and their father launched into a long explanation in which he vilified Arafat, the Palestinians and the Arabs. It included a series of clichés that I'd often heard: those Arabs, you can never trust them, give them an inch and they take a mile, the only thing they understand is the language of violence, and so on. We all listened in silence. Even

Stéphane's mother, who usually nodded her head in agreement with everything her husband said, sat perfectly still with her eyes glued to her plate. I threw Stéphane a few furtive glances, hoping he would interrupt and express his disagreement, but he didn't react either. And even though I'd always been so warmly welcomed into this family, I suddenly felt like a stranger. I was an intruder, betrayed because I had the feeling that we were all sharing this man's ideas, and betrayer because I'd never had the courage to fully open up to them about what I was. I was ashamed, I felt powerless, like a prisoner of this truncated image that I gave of myself. Dull anger was choking me; I barely managed to hold back my tears. I would have liked to shout, "What right do you have to talk against Arabs that way? What do you know about them? What makes you think you're worth more than they are?" I thought of my mother, who was beginning to suffer the first symptoms of her illness. By remaining silent, I was betraying her as well. I was angry at Stéphane and his family, but I was even angrier at myself because I was ashamed – ashamed of being an Arab and letting them insult me, ashamed of being Jewish and not having known how to respond to this man who was my kinsman.

Later, I often imagined myself explaining to Stéphane that my mother was Muslim, that she spoke to me in Arabic, that at my house, we celebrated Ramadan and Eid al-Fitr as well as Shabbat. I would take him aside after Hebrew class and tell him my story and my parents' story, about how they first met and about me being born. I would explain that they never married because religion prevented them from doing so but that they were above these differences and had found their sense of belonging elsewhere. No matter how many times I repeated this scenario in my head, I never found the right words. More importantly, I could never quite picture how he would react. I didn't trust him anymore.

After the long vacation, Mama was hospitalized and I never went back to the Sunday class. Stéphane didn't try to contact me and I didn't try to contact him.

＊

"What can I do for you?"

The man who had approached the table gave Daniel a gentle look that was a stark contrast to his imposing stature. He flashed a grin.

Daniel made a move as if to stand, shook the hand that Avner offered and invited him to sit down.

"I'm Daniel Benzaken. I'm Sara's father—"

Avner's faced darkened. Had Daniel touched his hand, he might have felt it trembling slightly, but Avner's expression quickly changed to a pained smile.

"Ah, I see."

"You know Sara?"

"Of course. We dated for a while."

Daniel studied Avner's face, his disarming smile. He didn't seem worried, but his look revealed a resigned sadness.

"You know that..."

Daniel hesitated. He didn't want to say, "Sara has disappeared." He didn't like the brutal, definitive nature of this affirmation. "Sara has disappeared" meant admitting that something had happened to her, that she was an accident victim, that she'd been attacked or kidnapped.

Avner took the lead. "Yes, I'm aware. A detective came to see me a few days ago."

"I thought you might know something, that she contacted you..."

"No, I haven't heard anything. I haven't seen her since we broke up... well, aside from a few meaningless phone calls."

"So you have no idea where she might be?"

Daniel went on without hesitating. "I'm sorry if I'm insisting... you understand... I feel like the investigation is going nowhere... and since you know Sara well?"

"But of course. I completely understand." Avner laid his hand on Daniel's arm in a reassuring, almost paternal way. "Sara and I parted on good terms but we haven't really stayed in touch."

Daniel shot Avner an inquisitive look, but aware that at any second their conversation could turn into an interrogation, he chose to remain silent. Once again, it was Avner who took the initiative.

"You want to know what happened between us, right?" Without giving Daniel a chance to answer, Avner gently patted his arm and quickly added, "No, no, it's okay, it's only natural. I can tell you this: Sara and I weren't made for each other. We were good friends... I still have a great deal of affection for her, you know. She has a lot of good qualities; she's very generous. But things were a bit complicated, too complicated for me. Sara asks herself a lot of questions; as they say, she's trying to 'find herself.' Me, I like the simple things. A family, kids, a good job... I don't ask for more. Sara... I don't think she really knows what she wants... and well, if you want my opinion, she keeps some strange company. Some people... quite frankly, they don't have a good influence on Sara. She deserves much better."

"What are you trying to say?"

"Listen, I don't want to say anything bad about anyone." Avner put his index finger to his lips, like a child repeating a nursery rhyme. "As we say in Hebrew, 'Lashon ha-rah' – slanderous talk." But after a moment's silence, he continued. "But... given the circumstances, I have to tell you... That Samira, a Palestinian... she's a strange girl. Sara used to talk about her with such fascination, like she was bewitched. Everything Samira said, her opinions, what she read, her political beliefs... Sara accepted everything she said, indiscriminately, with no critical evaluation at all. Listen, these are just my impressions. Maybe Sara has put some distance between them since then; we haven't spoken in several months."

"Do you know if Samira still lives on Mount Scopus?"

"I think so... But still you have to know... No, it's not my place... It's just conjecture, after all?"

"What do you want to say? What's it about?"

"The police didn't tell you about him?"

"About whom?"

"Well, about this guy, this Arab… He and Sara?"

"They did, in fact, mention her relationship with a Palestinian student. Is that the one you're talking about?"

"Maybe… All I know is that… Well, there've been rumours about him?"

"What kind rumours?"

"Well, you know, in Israel everything is complicated. How long have you been here?"

"I got here a little over a week ago. Why?"

Avner smiled. A smile that would have been condescending, were it not for the noticeable pain in it. The compassionate smile of a mother trying to comfort her 10-year-old son the first time his heart gets broken.

"Don't take this the wrong way, Mr. Benzaken, but you still have a lot to learn. This Palestinian guy, what do you know about him?"

"I… Not much, really. They took a class together at the university."

"Did Sara talk to you about him?"

"To tell the truth, no…"

"Doesn't that seem strange to you?"

"No… Well, I don't know. She doesn't have to tell me everything."

"Listen, Mr. Benzaken…"

Avner moved his glass aside, put his elbows on the table and leaned in toward Daniel. His voice was serious, restrained. "I don't know who this person is; I never met him. I've just heard that his family has been associated… let's just say… with suspicious activities. Believe me, I don't want to worry you unnecessarily. I clearly understand your situation. But if I were you, I'd try to find out more."

Not moving, Daniel stared out at the restaurant's terrace. His eyes followed the waitress, her brusque movements, her disingenuous smiles; he absorbed the last rays of the sun passing through the green and blue bottles on the tables as if through a stained-glass window; his eyes roamed distractedly over a tearful child who'd been refused an ice cream cone. But his mind absorbed none of these images. Daniel had no idea what to think anymore. Samira, Ibrahim, Avner... Whole chunks of Sara's life were slowly revealing themselves. During their phone calls, Sara spoke only about her courses and her research. Why hadn't he been more perceptive? Instead of talking about his painting, his lectures and his academic preoccupations, he should have been asking Sara more questions and inquiring about her friends, her social life, her love life. But Sara didn't like to share confidences, at least not on the telephone. Now he regretted not having come to see her in December. What difference would it have made if his leg was in a cast? He should have at least made the effort. He and Sara could have had some real conversations. He would have grown closer to her; he would have shared her everyday life. Had she been worried, he would have known it without being told. He might have been able to help or advise her.

"Ah, my dear Rachel!"

Approaching their table was a smiling young woman whose blond mane and sparkling teeth clashed so violently with her bronzed skin that she resembled a photograph's negative. Without standing, Avner put his arm around her waist and turned toward Daniel. "Mr. Benzaken, I'd like to introduce my fiancée, Rachel."

Daniel shook the woman's limp, moist hand and forced a smile of his own. Without further ado, he rose, thanked Avner and left the restaurant.

Night was falling. The laughter of couples with their arms around each other, the pounding of music coming from the bars, the mopeds buzzing between the cars surrounded Daniel, who for a moment let himself be pulled along by the ebb and flow of ordinary life as it bathed in the evening's lights.

The next day, Daniel would go to see Samira.

❋

Khirbet Qeiyafa, November 7, 2008
I've been at this archaeological site almost a week. They say that the ruins of the biblical city of Sha'arayim are buried here at Khirbet Qeiyafa. Shlomo, my research director, supervises the excavations. There are about 20 of us who have volunteered to work on the dig.

I never liked groups much and this one no more than the others, but I'm beginning to adjust to this ascetic existence, full of obligations and duties and almost completely lacking in free time. We get up at dawn, around 5:30 a.m., and all gather at the picnic tables for breakfast. We don't talk a lot. It's as if the night, like a holy place, imposes silence on us. We don't look at each other much either, maybe so that we don't have to admit we have nothing to say to each other. Then we clear the tables, some do the dishes, others dry, and 10 minutes later, we regroup a few metres from the site, where Shlomo gives us the instructions for the day.

We work in teams of two or three, and I'm often paired with Tamar, a girl my age who shares a tent with me at night. She's tall, slim and smiley – my complete opposite. Thanks to her, I've been able to get closer to the rest of the group. In the afternoon, when we gather to wash the pottery we've found during the day, I join the conversations. I don't know Hebrew well enough yet to understand everything, and if Tamar notices that I've missed a joke, she discreetly leans toward me to explain.

Khirbet Qeiyafa, November 10, 2008
In the evening, stretched out side by side in the tent, Tamar and I have long talks until sleep overcomes us. Little by little, I learned that Tamar also lost her mother when she was fourteen, that she had a boyfriend in Tel Aviv but felt that even before she left to study in Jerusalem, their story had almost come to an end. Two or three times, she mentioned Dov, one of the volunteers in the group. Tall and thin with unkempt hair, Dov has a joyful if somewhat teasing smile that belies the sadness in his eyes.

Tamar tried to sound detached when she asked me what I thought of him. I just smiled at her, and she smiled back. I was touched by this sign of trust.

Khirbet Qeiyafa, November 13, 2008
Tonight, we all sat around a campfire. Dov took out his guitar and started singing songs by the Beatles, the Rolling Stones and some Israeli singers that I didn't know. Every once in a while, Tamar would whisper their names in my ear: Yehuda Poliker, David Broza, Idan Raichel. One by one, the others joined in. I tried to hum along since I was familiar with a few of the songs, but my heart wasn't in it. I let myself drift and listened to the voices that were sometimes joyous, sometimes sad and dissonant. I listened as if I were a stranger who walks through a city at night and stops, trying to recognize the faint melodies playing in distant smoke-filled bars. I would have liked to do as the others did – smile, close my eyes, forget where I was – but I couldn't seem to step outside myself. I felt like the odd man out, like I was breaking the invisible thread that seemed to connect them all so well.

I got up and went to sit under a tree on the far side of the dig. The music was little more than a distant murmur, and the night's fragrant breeze was the only thing that, every now and then, disturbed the serenity of the place. Below my feet stretched the Valley of Elah. During the day, we could make out the villages, the stone houses and the olive trees, whose silvery leaves sparkled in the sun. I still felt that light, so close and vibrant, hiding in the darkness. It seemed that at any moment the fragile night would split apart to once again reveal all the colours of the day.

I looked up at the sky. I'd never seen so many stars. And in the silence slowly growing within me, I don't know why, but I began to think about Mama. For several years after her death, I refused to look at the pictures I had of her. I tried to imagine her face, to draw her features in my head, to repeat the scenes in which I sensed her happiness. I reconstructed the scenario of the flight we took together *every year to visit my grandparents in Paris. I was treated to a surprise each time – a box of crayons, a game of cards, a Lego car – and I impatiently waited to take our seats on the plane before finally being allowed to open my present. The year before her death, during Ramadan, we woke up at dawn to eat pita bread with hummus before fasting all day. And when I shut my eyes and concentrated very hard, I could still hear the plaintive tones of her voice, the way she slightly rolled the "r" in Sara whenever she said my name. For me, the most important thing wasn't having a lot of memories, but being certain that the ones I had were mine and not those of pale, frozen photographs come to take their place.*

Now, I try again to draw Mama's face in my head. But even when I close my eyes and forget the world around me, I fail. All I see is the image of a woman on her knees, her forehead touching the ground, prostrated in serene confidence and total abandon. At the height of her illness, Mama still prayed, despite her weakness and the nausea-inducing medications. When we visited her at the hospital in the evening, Papa and I often found the door to her room shut – a sign that she was praying. After a few minutes, she herself came to let us in and, hunched over, walked slowly back to her bed. Despite her bruised and broken body, her faced remained peaceful and her smile betrayed not the least bit of bitterness.

For a long time, I believed that Mama was praying for God to heal her. When she died, I was full of hate and anger. How could God abandon my mother when she had never failed, not even for a minute, to give Him her love and devotion? Why hadn't He heard my prayers? And why, above all else, had He ignored hers? It was then that God began to fade from my life.

✻

Rather than take the bus, Daniel decided to walk to the dorm on Mount Scopus. He hesitated for a moment at the building's door, then pressed the buzzer. A young woman answered the intercom, a vexed tone in her voice. Had he woken her? But it was already 10 o'clock in the morning. "Who's there?" Disconcerted, Daniel was ready to leave. The impatient, irritated voice insisted, "Who's there, already?"

Daniel finally answered, "It's... It's Daniel Benzaken. I'm the dad... Sara's father." A moment of silence was followed by the strident cry of the buzzer, which seemed to convey the woman's ill-humour.

He pushed the door open and climbed the stairs. Samira was waiting on the landing. At first, he saw only her eyes, set imposingly at the top of a gaunt face with hollow cheeks. They looked like two glistening black stones, the last vestiges of a sandcastle whose ramparts, towers and battlements had been devoured by the sea.

"I'm sorry... I didn't know it was you... Please, come in." Samira, barefoot and dressed in a housecoat, smiled timidly at Daniel like a child who was ashamed of having been insolent with her teacher. From the kitchen emanated the combined smells of coffee and lentil soup. "Please," Samira repeated as she indicated the door to the living room, "Come in and sit down. I'm going to get dressed. I'll just be a second." As he crossed the hall, Daniel stopped briefly in front of a half-open door. In the dim light, he could make out a desk piled high with books, a Charlie Chaplin poster, and on the back of a chair, the blue linen scarf Sara had been wearing the day she left Montreal.

"Don't stay there. Come sit down." The young woman smiled at him. She now wore a flowered cotton dress and had pulled her long black hair up into a bun. Daniel followed her into the living room. He tried to remember his conversation with Avner, Avner's allusions to Samira's political opinions and the bad influence she'd been on Sara. "I have to be on my guard, no matter what," he thought.

"Can I offer you something to drink?"

"No, thanks." Daniel sat on the sofa and Samira took a seat facing him.

"I'm glad you're here. I have to say... I've been worried about Sara... for a while now." Her rapid, breathless delivery split the words apart, fractured the phrases, obliterated whole portions of sentences, as if there were several contradictory voices doing battle within her.

"She didn't like to talk about it... but she did confide in me. She didn't tell you anything?"

"About what?"

"The telephone calls... the... lately, she was very scared?"

Daniel blanched. "I don't understand. What are you trying to tell me?"

"She was getting... anonymous phone calls. At first, she didn't think anything of it. She thought the calls would eventually stop, but they kept coming. All day long. Late at night. And then there were some letters, too."

"What letters?"

"Anonymous letters. Hate mail."

"But... Why didn't she go to the police?"

"She did. But I don't think they took her seriously. You should talk to the police officer, the one in charge of the investigation."

"Detective Ben-Ami?"

"Yes. Monday – it was over two weeks ago – I was worried because I hadn't seen Sara. Normally, when she spends the week-end with Ibrahim, she comes back Sunday evening. I called her several times, of course, and left messages, but she didn't call me back. And that's not her style, you know, she would have let me know... Even if she'd gone away with Ibrahim and didn't want anyone to know where they were, she would have at least returned my calls. No, really, it's very weird..."

Daniel turned toward the half-open window. A warm breeze brought in odours from the street: grilled meat and carbon dioxide. The distant rumble of cars, like the sound of the ocean, told a thousand stories, a thousand little disconnected dramas, pitiful reflections of his own confusion.

His eyes met Samira's. The questions jockeyed for position in his mind, each one generating 10 others, a branching tree weighted with interrogations, doubts and suspicions that overlapped and became entangled. Why hadn't the policeman mentioned the anonymous letters? Who could have threatened Sara? He remembered the man asking him if Sara had any enemies. At the time, he'd thought the question absurd, but now Daniel realized that Detective Ben-Ami knew more than he was letting on. Why had Ben-Ami hidden the truth from him? And could he trust Samira? Could she have made up the story about anonymous letters? But why would she?

"Please excuse me," said Samira. "I have to go to class now." She stood and walked Daniel to the door. On the landing, she put a hand on his shoulder. It was meant to be reassuring, but Daniel could not keep himself from shuddering. This very gentle contact penetrated him for a brief moment, reminding him of his unbearable solitude.

"Call me after you've spoken to the detective again. I still have a lot to tell you…"

❋

From: Sara
To: Daniel
Subject: Back to Jerusalem
Friday, November 14, 2008, 10:12 p.m.

Good evening, Papa!
I just got back from Khirbet Qeiyafa.
Long days of strenuous work. I'm stiff and I ache all over! But it did me good to empty my mind a bit after all these weeks with my nose in the books. At first, I wasn't very comfortable with the group. Even if I'm making progress with Hebrew, I still have trouble following conversations, especially when everyone is talking at the same time. But after a week, I got used to it.

The last night, we all sat around a campfire singing songs. One of the volunteers, a Canadian from Vancouver, brought marshmallows and showed everyone how to roast them over the fire. The taste of burnt sugar reminded me of our vacations in Maine. Remember? At night, on the beach, you also had us enjoy the taste of burnt marsh-mallows.

As you can see, it doesn't take much these days to send me down the slippery slope of memories.

I'll call you tomorrow.

Kisses,

Sara

※

Jerusalem, November 16, 2008

His eyes, from the other side of the restaurant, were glued to me. I didn't meet his gaze, but when I turned my face toward him – furtively, so I wouldn't give him the impression that I'd noticed his little game – I think I detected a smile. Thinking about it more carefully now, perhaps it wasn't a smile but more of an expression of satisfaction, as if he already knew how things would turn out.

My friends from Khirbet Qeiyafa took me there. Back in Jerusalem after two weeks of hard work, they decided to celebrate, even if the excavations hadn't revealed much of anything useful yet: a few fragments of urns, burnt olive pits, all sorts of finds that look more like the random objects you'd find in a kid's pocket than treasures holding the key to the past.

Tonight, I sat between Dov and Tamar. I tried to follow their animated conversation but, in spite of myself, I was more interested in their facial expressions, the inflections of their voices, especially their gestures, which seemed a bit exaggerated to me, as if they were fencing with each other across the table. It was one of those endless discussions whose purpose is more to prove that you're right than to learn what the other person really thinks. Dov claimed that true infidelity happens in the heart, that having a one-night stand with a woman isn't really cheating on the one you love. It's only when you fall in love with someone else, even if it's never more than a platonic relationship, that you're really cheating. Tamar argued to the contrary. In her opinion, making love is the most intimate act possible, the one in which we fully reveal ourselves, even when we find little pleasure in it, and that when we give ourselves to someone else, it's as if we've taken away from the loved one everything he'd been promised. I watched them and followed the movements of their hands, which jousted before my eyes and came as close together as they could without actually touching, and I said to myself that they were probably keeping this argument going only to make their mating dance last a bit longer.

A few metres from our table, his face half-hidden by the long stems of a bouquet of lilies, the man continued to watch me. His black eyebrows made him look severe, but his lips kept promising the beginning of a smile. Still staring at me, he talked to the friends seated with him, just like a head chef who fully focuses on his sauce while continuing to watch his assistants' progress out of the corner of his eye.

When it came time to leave, my friends suggested that we go have a drink at a bar in Nahalat Shiva, but I was too tired and wanted to go back to my room. I had just turned the corner when I heard a voice behind me calling to me. "Excuse me! You there!" I turned around. It was the man from the restaurant. I looked at him in confusion. He seemed shorter than he had earlier. His big shoulders, his pleasant look and his stomach, which already showed early indications of a potbelly, made him appear both imposing and reassuring. "I noticed that you were alone… Wouldn't you like me to see you home?" Maybe I should have ignored him or pretended I didn't understand. But maybe because of his open and generous smile, I felt obligated to reply. "No, thanks, I can make it back on my own." He didn't seem surprised nor did he seem inclined to leave.

"I was watching you earlier, in the restaurant… Are you French?"

I didn't want to get involved in the conversation but it was too late. In a disgruntled tone, I answered him while quickly turning away to see if the bus was coming, "No… I'm from Montreal."

Unperturbed, he continued to smile. "Montreal! I love Montreal!" And he proceeded to list all the places he'd visited there: the Old Port, Saint-Louis Square, the Botanical Garden… Noticing my indifference to this, he persisted, "Are you a student here?"

I simply nodded my head. "At Hebrew U?" I nodded again. I was quite relieved to see the bus approaching at last. As I was climbing aboard, I took a last glance in his direction, less to excuse my coldness than to check the expression on his face. He was still smiling, though a bit more timidly than before.

Once back on Mount Scopus, I headed straight to my room. Samira was already asleep. I went to the kitchen to drink a glass of water and then I brushed my teeth. In the half-light, I felt as if he were still observing me, as if he had settled his sight on me, like a caress upon my shoulder or like a stain that I alone could see. Perhaps my efforts to push him away had left a hollowness in me, an empty space that his presence had, quite naturally, come to fill. I almost regretted not having trusted him.

Jerusalem, November 17, 2008
Van Gogh exhibit in Tel Aviv. A group of eight-to-ten-year-old kids, sitting on the floor in front of Sunflowers. *Their teacher asked what they thought about the painting. Finally, one little boy answered, "I think it's pretty, but there's too much yellow. Way too much yellow."*

Jerusalem, November 18, 2008
I glued a few posters to the wall in my room: Charlie Chaplin sitting on a bench with a white flower in his hand, a reproduction of The Starry Night *by Van Gogh, an ancient map of Jerusalem. I sat on my bed to consider the result. It's a little weird to see these images from my familiar surroundings on Édouard-Montpetit, from Montreal,*

transplanted here to Jerusalem and this little room with its white walls bathed in light.

My eyes linger on The Starry Night. *The deep blue, rich and full of warmth, sends me back to the distant past. It reminds me of a place, a conversation perhaps, but I can't put my finger on it.*

To retrace this memory, I'd have to abandon my usual landmarks: the familiar places, my school, the streets of the Côte-des-Neiges neighbourhood, our chalet in Saint-Adolphe. I would have to search my memory for those paths that lead us toward unexpected visions, like desire paths: those improvised shortcuts that can be found in certain parks, created by hikers determined to carve out new trails. The past has its marked trails, too: the cities, the dates, the vacation photos, the memory's official cartography. And then there are the invented pathways, the renegade routes that send us off in pursuit of an odour, a face whose features we can scarcely define, a colour worn by a throng of unknown voices. In the end, it is these paths of desire that, unbeknownst to us, guide us through the past and maintain the fabric of our memory.

Jerusalem, November 18, 2008, 11:15 p.m.
I persist, I continue to sift through my past, and in this futile race toward the memories where my imagination reigns supreme, I am no longer sure of anything.

Maybe this is the same blue I saw at dawn, when Mama woke me up for breakfast during the month of Ramadan. She would sit me at the white kitchen table and I'd watched her prepare our food. I close my eyes and piece by piece, the scene unfolds again: the half-open window admitting swells of night air that is sometimes warm and humid, sometimes cool and fragrant; the diaphanous light of the neons giving my mother's hands a sepulchral pallor as they busily cut fruit on the counter; the impatient cries of birds that flit from tree to tree like a single breath, anxious and erratic. Mama joins me at the table and insists that I finish my fruit, even if the oranges are so tart that I can't help grimacing.

At such times, we spoke little, but Mama willingly answered my questions. Her explanations were nothing like the categorical affirmations that my grandmother drummed into me whenever we visited her in Paris: "We fast to remind ourselves of those who are hungry." Or even better, "We follow the Prophet's example. Fasting brings us closer to him." Quite the contrary, Mama began the answer to each of my questions by saying she didn't know. Then she would elaborate: "What I think is of no value. Our actions are what matter above all else. When you pray, when you fast, you draw the presence of God around you. It's only an image; maybe there's nothing behind it. But as long as you occupy this space, as long as the image exists, God remains possible."

That year, Ramadan had started in July, and during the long days of fasting, I went to the pharmacy with Mama to lend her a hand. While she updated customers' files, she sent me to look for boxes of pills and tubes of cream. I walked between the high shelves, examining the myriad white labels, all perfectly aligned. They gave off the humid smell of newsprint, a clinical coolness that contrasted with the warmth of my mother's velvety voice. We returned home in the evening to a copious meal that Papa had prepared for us – lentil soup, chicken with rice, stuffed eggplant, and for dessert, baklava flavoured with orange blossom. He sat at the table with us and ate with such appetite that I wondered if he was fasting too, to show his solidarity.

All these memories come back to me like visions of an unclouded happiness. The school year had ended and I was free of my books, notebooks and lessons to be learned. I was free, I was mistress of my time: two long months to read as I pleased, walk without purpose and sleep in late. Today, I am jealous of this past, as if it had never belonged to me, as if it had been someone else's happiness. But if I long for these moments, it's not because I want to relive them. Nostalgia is not a yearning for the past but a desire for eternity. What we miss is not primarily the joy or lightness that we felt, but the infinite plenitude of our feelings, closed to time and impervious *to change. It's the eternal texture of the moment, captured in the rough stone of life, detached from its future.*

⁂

From: Daniel
To: Sara
Subject: Mama
Wednesday, November 19, 2008, 6:16 p.m.

Dearest daughter,

Yesterday was the anniversary of your mother's death. It was the first time I'd gone to the cemetery without you, and naturally with my terrible sense of direction, I got lost. I had to ask the way several times before finding it.

The other day, I had dinner with a colleague, Georges Lamoureux. You've met him, I think; he's a specialist in antiquity. Again he offered to introduce me to someone, a CEGEP professor, very pretty, a movie fanatic. According to Georges, she's too smart and that's why she's still single. He really pushed me to meet her and even suggested organizing a dinner at his house. I finally had to gently tell him that I really wasn't interested.

People who live with their significant other sometimes have a hard time imagining that a person might choose to remain single – because it's exactly that fear of solitude that threw them into the arms of the other in the first place. As I've often told you, I'm no hero: it's not fidelity to your mother that keeps me celibate, but laziness. It's because now that I've finally managed to surround myself with everything I need to live, I haven't the strength, the desire or the imagination necessary to remodel my little burrow.

I have my plane ticket. I arrive in Jerusalem on December 22. Can't wait to see you.

Your loving papa

When he reached the street, Daniel grabbed his cell phone and dialled Detective Ben-Ami's number. For once, the policeman answered. Daniel tried as best he could to suppress his anger.

"Why didn't you tell me anything?"

"About what?"

"Don't play innocent. You know perfectly well what I want to talk about."

"Mr. Benzaken, let me assure you—"

"Anonymous letters! Are you trying to tell me you're not aware of this?"

"Uh… I… listen?"

"Why didn't you say something? Is there anything else you're hiding from me?"

"Mr. Benzaken, you misunderstand, believe me. I simply wanted to save you needless worry… The letters… There's nothing to prove they have anything to do with your daughter's disappearance—"

"Perhaps, but you must admit that it's still strange, no? Do you know where those letters came from? You've had them analyzed, right?"

"Of course. But they're only one of the leads we want to follow. For the moment, we have to consider all hypotheses, including the possibility that Sara decided to leave on her own, without advising anyone."

"What are you insinuating?"

"These things do happen. More often than you may think. A broken heart, a period of depression… Sometimes, even their loved ones haven't a clue."

Detective Ben-Ami paused, as if he wanted to verify the effect his words were having on Daniel.

"I understand your concern, Mr. Benzaken. But have no fear, we are availing ourselves of all possible resources. Patience, Mr. Benzaken. Have patience, that's all I can tell you."

Jerusalem, November 21, 2008
I just finished reading Elias Khoury's Gate of the Sun. *Hope, saved*
by the entangled tales that never cease to be born and to name:
"The human being reveals his name only at the moment of his
disappearance, in other words, when his name becomes a shroud."

Jerusalem, November 23, 2008
I feel a bit disoriented tonight. I have an essay to hand in tomorrow
but the ideas aren't flowing. I go from one book to another, I reread
my notes – nothing to be done about it, I've lost my train of thought.
And worst of all, I'm not too worried about it. I'll go see my professor
tomorrow morning, explain that I was sick and ask for a few days'
extension.

In spite of myself, I think about the man from the restaurant. But
the next time we see each other – if indeed he chooses to remember
me – I'll never succeed in finding him as good-looking as he is in my
imagination. I'll be disappointed. I'll see his nose that's a bit too
strong, his sad eyes, his oily cheeks, his jug-ears and I'll say to myself:
no, really, he is clearly not all that appealing. And yet I will let myself
listen to the sound of his voice, I will discover his talent as a story-
teller, I will convince myself that behind his sleepy eyes lurk the
hidden treasures of goodness and grace.

When I abandoned him at the bus stop last week, I didn̦'t think
I'd ever see him again. But the day before yesterday, as I was walking
to the movie theatre, I heard a voice behind me. I turned around and
there he was, standing at the corner of the street that leads to
Mishkenot Sha'ananim, waving wildly at me with an innocent smile
lighting up his face. How had he gotten there? Had he followed me?
Was this really a coincidence?

He crossed the street and held out his hand, beaming and asking,
"Do you remember me?" It was more a statement than a question. "It's
strange, don't you think? I was coming back from my parents' place

and boom, here you are! I don't want to bother you, but… Can I invite you for a drink?" I said that I was going to see a movie, but after, maybe, or perhaps another day… He smiled at me; he must have thought I was trying to get rid of him. But instead of beating a retreat, he gave me a defiant look and replied, "Okay. I have a few errands to do in the neighbourhood. I'll wait for you in the café over there on the corner." I stood there speechless; I didn't know how to react. I should have had the presence of mind to say I already had plans, that I had to have dinner with a girlfriend or that I had a presentation to prepare for the next day. But I simply acquiesced, like a child summoned to come inside at the appointed hour.

Sitting in the back of the theatre, I couldn't stop thinking about this stranger whose name I didn't even know. I was annoyed with myself for not having been firmer with him, but his insistence had left me flustered. I wasn't used to that sort of thing. The boys I'd known in Montreal hadn't been quite so pushy.

Throughout the entire film, I wondered how I might extricate myself from the situation. First, I tried to convince myself that he wouldn't show up. But that was fairly unlikely, considering the determination he had shown. So I pictured myself with him at the café: I would be polite but no more than that, I would ask him questions but not too many, I would be distracted but not to the point where he would think me indifferent.

When I left the theatre, I headed toward the café he had pointed out. He wasn't there. I was about to turn back, half-relieved, when I felt a hand on my shoulder. I turned around. He looked at me and gave me a big smile. "I hope I didn't scare you. You look surprised. Did you think I wouldn't be here to meet you? Come on, you can tell me the truth, I won't be mad." His expression showed a candour I hadn't noticed before.

We walked toward Nahalat Shiva. Night was falling and people were milling about the streets. From time to time, his arm brushed mine. I was afraid he would take my hand.

At the restaurant, he became more animated. I learned that his name was Avner, that he was 29 and that he managed one of his father's restaurants. I had just come out of that very restaurant – The Djerba Palace – when he approached me the other day. I listened to him describe his daily routine, his admiration for his father, who had "slaved all his life for his family," and I couldn't help thinking that this wasn't the first time he'd told this story. With the same artificial emotion and the same somewhat exaggerated gestures, he clearly had tried to seduce a number of girls before me, convinced that this image of stability and harmony would be enough to lead them into his arms.

The streets were empty when we left the restaurant. I heard his voice echoing in the humid evening air, without trying too hard to follow the thread of his story. It was something about a new restaurant in Tel Aviv, a childhood friend he'd found again, his older sister who had just gotten engaged.

When it came time to say goodbye, he leaned in toward me. I felt him hesitating but I didn't give him the chance to decide. I put my hand firmly on his shoulder, planted a quick kiss on his cheek and went into my building without looking back.

I immediately felt relieved. But now that I'm alone, I regret having done everything I could to keep him at a distance. I'm sure he won't be calling me.

Jerusalem, November 27, 2008

He called, in spite of everything. He had tickets for a jazz concert at a "very exclusive" club in Tel Aviv. He came to pick me up in a car – his father's convertible – and we stopped at The Djerba Palace before getting underway. The employees all greeted him with an energetic "Hey, boss!" but I detected silent suspicion in their overly bright smiles. The waitresses exchanged knowing looks when Avner passed by them. They kept their own counsel for the moment, but I was sure that as soon as we left, the nasty jokes would start to fly.

A minor incident was all it took to show me the reason for this hostility. One of the waitresses, a young woman with an ample

*derrière and a small face, was hurrying to clear the table in the back
so she could come to take our order. In her haste, she knocked over a
coffee cup and its contents splashed onto a customer's white blouse.
The woman leaped up and yelled, "Stupid girl! Can't you be more
careful?!" Everyone turned around. Red with shame, the young
waitress vainly offered a napkin to the client, a hefty woman with
heavy makeup who was glaring angrily at her. She continued to
reprimand the waitress, claiming that her brand-new blouse was
ruined and demanding immediate compensation.*

*Avner quickly took charge. With a scornful wave, he banished the
waitress and with his head bent to the lady's ear, he began negotiating
with her. I didn't hear their discussion, but after a few minutes, the
lady smiled at him and gratefully accepted the hand he held out to
her. Once the situation had been resolved, he menacingly walked over
to the waitress, grabbed her by the arm, digging his fingers into her
plump white flesh, and silently led her into the kitchen. As soon as
the door closed, I could hear Avner's voice as he thundered at the
young woman. She tried to respond, to explain herself, her voice
choked by sobs, but Avner wouldn't listen to her and continued his
brutal tongue-lashing. Embarrassed, the restaurant's customers took
refuge in their whispered conversations. Avner soon returned to the
dining room, his face serene, his expression triumphant. As he passed
close to me, he patted my shoulder as if he'd just protected me from
great danger.*

*Back in the car, Avner became very chatty. He took pleasure in
describing the practical jokes that he and his friends played on their
schoolmates. He bragged about his bad grades, imitated his history
teacher's reedy voice, took a sanctimonious tone to make fun of the
smartest boy in the class, a sickly crybaby who had become, according
to Avner, nothing more than a modest bank employee. I docilely
listened to him and, being a good audience, I deliberately laughed at
his jokes. But I couldn't help thinking about the young waitress with
her delicate features and tear-filled eyes. I looked at Avner and
couldn't reconcile his cheerful voice, that awkward charm, with the*

savage rant he had inflicted on the young woman just a few minutes
earlier. From time to time, he turned toward me and, despite his kind,
gentle smile, I saw only a contorted face full of aggression and rage.

❈

Daniel had been walking the shady streets of Yemin Moshe for over an hour. He walked without purpose, to exhaust himself, to exhaust his thoughts. These thoughts, creating an invisible undertow, drew him irresistibly out to sea, into an immense and pathless past. Now he sees himself, panic-stricken and out of breath, striding up and down the streets of Old Montreal. He goes down Saint-Sulpice and turns onto Saint-Paul. At Place Royale, he stops for a minute, looks in every direction and then goes back up Rue de la Capitale. "Sara! Sara!" He calls her with all his strength, until his voice is hoarse. So what if passersby look at him, disconcerted, as if he were a lunatic? He has to find Sara, it is imperative that he find her... hoping... hoping only that nothing has happened to her!

He stops someone in front of the Pointe-à-Callière Museum. "Have you seen a little girl? She's five years old, wearing a light-blue cap..." Dumbfounded, the woman stutters out a few jumbled words. Daniel doesn't try to understand; he resumes his frantic running, jostling, stomping, stumbling, shouting: "Sara! Sara!" Le Bourlingueur, St-François-Xavier Street, Place d'Youville – no, it's impossible, she couldn't have gone this far. They'd been waiting in line at the ice cream stand at the corner of Saint-Dizier when Sara stepped away to look at the kites in a toy-store window. He had only taken his eyes off her for a second, the time it took to pay for her cone, and she had disappeared. Breathless, his forehead covered in sweat, Daniel now goes back up Rue Saint-Paul. Already he is thinking, "I have to find a telephone, I have to call the police." And then finally, back on Saint-Dizier, he sees Sara waiting by the ice cream stand. A lady wearing a big straw hat is squatting down beside her and talking to her, her mouth lightly touching her ear and a hand resting lightly on her shoulder. Before letting her run to meet her father, she plants a kiss on her cheek that leaves behind a scarlet bird the colour of her lipstick. Sara isn't crying. She holds her arms out to Daniel, lets him pick her up and presses her pale face into his neck.

Back home, Daniel doesn't dare tell Leila about the incident, and Sara follows him in his lie. "How was your afternoon?"

Giving Sara a knowing look, Daniel hastens to reply, "Well, great, it was really great. Right, Sara?" Is Leila fooled? She notices the red bird on her daughter's cheek but simply takes a handkerchief and wipes her face clean. Then she raises her eyes to Daniel. It is a look that means to say, "I trust you."

It was the same expression, both stern and pleading, that he now saw as he imagined Leila walking beside him down the streets of Jerusalem or watching him washing up in his hotel room. This responsibility in which she enveloped him, like a patient who puts his life into a surgeon's hands, choked him, shackled him, and anchored to each one of his acts the shadow of an evil omen.

❊

From: Sara
To: Daniel
Subject: Again
Friday, November 28, 2008, 8:43 p.m.

Hi, Papa.
I was tempted to tell you about it on the phone last weekend, but I decided it was a bit premature. I actually have met someone. His name is Avner. He's from Tel Aviv but lives in Jerusalem. He manages one of his father's restaurants. He has a certain charm and we get along well, and for now, that's enough for me.
He's told me a bit about his life. His father was born in Tunis and came from nothing but little by little, he began to acquire restaurants in Tel Aviv, Jaffa and Jerusalem. Avner studied law and then

went to work with his father. He's very ambitious and talks about "building a small empire."

He's very nice, very attentive, but I don't know if it'll go any further.

Anyway, I'll tell you more when we speak in a couple of days.

Have a good night.

Sara

❅

Jerusalem, November 30, 2008

Yesterday, for the first time, Avner asked me about my parents. After a long walk through the streets of Netanya, we decided to spend an hour at the beach before heading back to Jerusalem. Sitting and looking at the waves, elbows buried in the sand, I felt his hand touch mine as if by accident, like a casual gesture repeated a thousand times. I let him do it, less because I was touched by this show of intimacy than because I didn't want to make him uncomfortable.

When he learned my father had been born in Morocco, his face suddenly lit up and he began to list the names of all the Moroccans he'd been friends with since elementary school: Benamron, Amzallag, Malka, Abitbol, Toledano, Benzaken, Azoulay. Noticing that his knowledge of Moroccan genealogy was of little interest to me, he asked me about my mother. I told him she was Lebanese and that she had left Beirut with her parents during the civil war. But I didn't tell him she was Muslim.

Why did I hide the truth from him? What kind of game was I playing? I should have been more honest, not so much for him but for myself. Was I afraid of his reaction? Had I revealed my mother's background, he surely would have looked at me in alarm. I would have suddenly been transformed from confidante to intruder. I would have been the enemy who'd been unmasked. But how could I be so sure? Why hadn't I trusted him? I think I was afraid. Afraid he would reject me. Because, despite my hesitations, even if I'm still not sure what I feel for him, I don't want to be alone again.

So that I could be with Avner, I created a unified image of myself, smoothing out all its rough edges and cleansing it of all that seemed disagreeable and heavy to me. And for me to match this image, I had to lop off an entire part of who and what I am. With Avner, I experience the pleasure of living without questions and above all, of living with the security – no matter how illusory – of belonging. As far as he's concerned, I'm just a Jewish girl from Montreal, nothing else. In the eyes of his old army buddies and his cousins with whom we had Shabbat dinner on Friday night, I am "one of theirs." I feel united in solidarity, without wondering too much about what cause I am joining or toward which destiny I am allowing myself to be led.

How is it that it costs me so little to hide who I am? Doesn't that mean that when I nonchalantly declare myself to be Jewish and Muslim, I'm being just as insincere? Isn't this double affiliation that I have previously claimed without serious consideration of the consequences just another smokescreen? A category, unique perhaps but shallow too, that I somewhat frivolously offer up to others without too much thought, in an effort to be provocative? It's a way to make myself interesting without really sharing much about myself. It's putting all the questions that torment me aside and being satisfied, as if I too were being fooled, with pale images of myself, invented and redesigned to fit the circumstances.

Jerusalem, December 3, 2008
Avner kissed me. It was neither good nor bad. I didn't feel elevated, transported or lost in time but I wasn't disgusted either. I thought of his moist hands, his thick, fleshy arms pulling me toward him, his scratchy chin against my cheek.

After a long walk through the streets of Tel Aviv, we ended up at a jazz bar where the great trumpeter Avishai Cohen was performing. I watched Avner gently move to the sound of the music, his eyes closed, while I wondered if the virtuoso's strident trills were going to destroy my eardrums. From time to time, Avner looked at me and I

*responded with a smile, which was probably less sincere than I would
have liked. I stuffed myself with tacos and salted peanuts.*

*We left around midnight (I tried to disguise my relief) and Avner
came back to Mount Scopus with me. As we were about to go our
separate ways, he leaned toward me. I knew what was going to
happen. I could have gently pushed him away and left him there with
a chaste kiss on the cheek, but I didn't have the heart. So without
pleasure, I did as he wished. I closed my eyes and let his lips touch
mine. I felt his clumsy but determined tongue, his shallow breathing,
his potbelly pressing against me. When he released his grip, his eyes –
full of passion and solicitude – were studying my face. I found it
moving. I was far from feeling love or desire, but at least I had finally
given something of myself. Climbing the stairs to my room, I felt
lighter, as you do after you've just completed a somewhat arduous task
that you've put off far too long. It was only once I was lying in my
bed, shivering under the damp sheets, that my cloud returned and
with it, the confused realization that the next time, I'd probably have
to go further.*

❋

From: Daniel
To: Sara
Subject: Little hitch
Friday, December 5, 2008, 11:16 a.m.

Dear Sara,
I left a message on your cell phone a little earlier today. Please don't
worry, but I wanted to tell you that I slipped on the sidewalk and fell
this morning, near the house. There was black ice and I was in a
hurry and wasn't paying attention.
The annoying part is that I broke my ankle. I just got back from the
hospital. They put me in a cast for five weeks.
I think I might have to cancel my trip to Jerusalem. I want to be

with you so badly, but I think I'll have a hard time travelling with crutches.

So I'll come in May.

Big hug,

Papa

P.S. I was glad you told me a bit about Avner on the phone the other day. I'm anxious to hear more.

From: Sara

To: Daniel

Subject: Little hitch

Friday, December 5, 2008, 11:40 a.m.

Papa, I just read your email. I'm so disappointed.

I'd started a list of all the places I wanted to show you. I would have liked to introduce you to my friends, especially Samira. Anyway, we'll save it for another time.

I'm going to have dinner with Samira's parents tonight. I'll call you tomorrow.

Take care of yourself!

Sara

❁

Jerusalem, December 5, 2008

Samira invited me to have supper tonight at her parents' house in the Bab al-Zahra neighbourhood. We took the bus and got off to buy flowers on Salah-al-Din Street. Some of the merchants had already closed their shops to go to the mosque. Along the dusty roads, we ran into scattered groups of teenagers playing soccer and busy women leading a child with one hand and pushing a baby carriage with the other. The low houses emitted an aroma of fresh bread, cinnamon and cardamom.

For the occasion, Samira had worn a headscarf. Her parents knew that she had given up going to the mosque a long time ago, but it was understood that she would make an effort to prove to her uncles, cousins and the rest of the family that she was still a "good Muslim girl."

Samira did not make a habit of bringing friends to meet her parents. Because of the comments and criticisms of her father – she should become a lawyer like him; nothing would prevent her from writing poetry in her free time, if she so desired, but at least she would have a real profession – she had learned to compartmentalize her life and shelter the student aspect of it from her family's prying eyes. I am the most "presentable" of her friends, the one who raises the least suspicion about the immense chasm between her true aspirations and the dreams that her parents still harbour for her.

But I still had to be prepared. So Samira started reeling off the topics of conversation that could not be broached in her father's presence: career plans (in his opinion, archaeology was worth little more than poetry), the arts, literature and film (useless activities that give rise only to hubris or disappointment), politics, of course (whatever position Samira takes, her father always does his best to contradict her: sometimes Arafat was duped in Oslo and sometimes he was a fine strategist; one day Mahmoud Abbas is the American's vassal and the next day he's the Palestinians only hope), and above all, boys must never be discussed.

Since starting at the university, Samira had had a few love affairs, and she never tried to hide her displeasure whenever her mother or aunt suggested introducing her to a young man from a "good family." For one semester, she had even dated a Jewish student, an American from Boston who had come to finish his doctorate in theology at Hebrew University in Jerusalem. Her father had caught wind of it – she never knew how – and she had been forced to break it off immediately. His name was Michael Weiss, and when Samira said his name, her voice held a mixture of mischief, resentment and melancholy.

This confession was the pretext I was waiting for. Her admission allowed me to come right out and tell her my story, my parents' story: Mama's exile and how she met my father, a Moroccan Jewish immigrant. Samira turned toward me, incredulous. Then her face brightened, as if she'd just been recognized, as if she'd found in me an unexpected ally. She wanted to know everything: how their families had reacted, how they had raised me, what each one had taught me. I was touched by her curiosity and surprised to note that she wasn't angry with me for not having confided in her sooner. Naturally, this revelation remained our secret. But I felt that by bringing me into her home, she was scoring one more victory over her unsuspecting parents.

Throughout the entire meal, Samira cast me mischievous looks. She observed me as if she alone could see me, as if all the others – her parents, her older brother, her aunt – had been blind to my presence. From time to time, she watched her father out of the corner of her eye; it was as if she both hoped and feared that he would learn the truth. I myself remained apprehensive. I kept expecting him to ask me a personal question: "What does your father do? Do you still have family in Lebanon? What are your plans for the future?" Samira's father is small in stature with eyes deeply set in their sockets, pale skin and slack, almost beardless cheeks: he's not someone who makes much of an impression. But despite the meagreness and weakness of his features, you could read an anxious determination in his face, a powerful desire to penetrate the other and expose his secret thoughts.

Despite my fears, the conversation, which was punctuated with long silences, remained dull and free of pitfalls. After supper, Samira and I went to her room to get a few books. As we were leaving, her father shook my hand and said, "Come back and see us, please feel at home here." He wasn't smiling, but the earlier coldness in his face had given way to a shy benevolence.

Outside, the wind had picked up. Near Al-Hariri Street, we walked along the Rockefeller Garden from which emanated a fresh mist perfumed with the fertile scent of eucalyptus and spruce. Samira had slipped her arm under mine. In the deep darkness, I couldn't make out her face but I imagined she was smiling. In the silence, I felt that this evening had brought us closer together and put a bit more distance between her and her family.

※

Samira had told Daniel to meet her at the theatre coffee shop in the Yemin Moshe neighbourhood. He had already been waiting for her for half an hour. He looked at his watch and then at the paper on which he had written the address. No, he had definitely not made a mistake. Finally, he heard a voice, short of breath, behind him and felt a hand brush his shoulder.

"I'm sorry, the bus didn't come. I ended up taking a taxi. But the traffic at this hour…"

Her chignon had come undone and the sweat glued short black curls to her forehead, making her resemble a Roman shepherd.

"So," she hurriedly asked, "Did you speak to the detective again?"

"Yes."

"And?"

"He acted like he didn't want to worry me. To tell you the truth, I don't think the police are taking this very seriously."

"Maybe they're waiting to have more to go on."

"You think so? But it's been over two weeks…"

Daniel stopped speaking. He looked off into the distance, beyond the white stone of Yemin Moshe. After a long silence, he began again.

"I must tell you – I met Sara's ex-boyfriend, Avner. Do you know him?"

Samira smiled. "Yes, a bit. I'm sure he didn't have anything nice to say about me…"

"No, in fact, he didn't. What does he have against you?"

"It's complicated… But in short, he thinks that it's because of me that it didn't work out between the two of them."

"He thinks you influenced her?"

"Yes. But the truth is that Sara was never in love with him. The first time she told me about Avner, it was almost as if she was ashamed of him. He wasn't her type at all, but she thought he was nice. I think she probably found him touching; she was surprised by the interest he was showing in her. At first, he was very pleasant. Very attentive. A perfect gentleman. Eating out, concerts, little gifts… It's hard to resist all that. But at the end of the day, it's not enough. There has to be a spark, a little mystery… Sara figured it out. She didn't need me to tell her."

"So she was the one who ended it?"

"Yes, of course."

Daniel frowned.

"I get the feeling you don't believe me… Oh, I get it! That's obviously not what Avner told you. He must have said that they realized they weren't right for each other and that they split up 'by mutual agreement.' I'm not surprised. He actually took their break-up pretty badly."

"Did he try to change her mind?"

"Yes, you could say that. At first he left her alone. You would have thought he'd forgotten all about her, that he'd turned the page. But a few weeks later, he started calling her again. He insisted on seeing her again; he wanted to explain himself. It wasn't long at all before the calls took a menacing tone. He called very late at night and if she didn't answer, he'd keep on calling, until Sara was finally forced to turn off her phone."

"He knew that Sara was with Ibrahim?"

"Yes. I don't know how he found out because Sara never told him about Ibrahim. She suspected him of following her. And then the anonymous phone calls started. And the letters."

"Do you think Avner could be capable of—"

"I don't know. I don't know him well, but I can tell you he's the unpredictable type. He can be friendly and charming and the next minute, no one knows why, but he's in a fit of rage…"

Samira looked at Daniel. His face was ashen, his forehead covered in sweat, and his fingers trembled slightly.

"C'mon, it'll be okay, you'll see."

Empty words, words that can be found in every language and that, in one language or another, carry the same hollow weight. But it was Samira's voice that comforted him. That was all she was: a voice, a bit of life come to curl up against his, like an animal in the night.

※

Jerusalem, December 8, 2008
Beautiful production of Tom Stoppard's play, Rozencrantz *and* Guildenstern Are Dead, *at the university theatre. It's a bit too cerebral but it's full of gems. My favourite line: "Life is a gamble, at terrible odds – if it was a bet you wouldn't take it." Yes, but isn't it precisely because we didn't choose to be born that we cling so tightly to life?*

Jerusalem, December 9, 2008
I told Samira about my encounter with Avner. It was like a revelation. From the first words I spoke, as soon as I said his name, I had to admit the truth: I am not in love. All my questioning, my hesitations, my efforts to see him as handsome, sexy and tender-hearted were nothing more than an elaborate but futile exercise to invent feelings I don't have. And it didn't take Samira long to figure it out. "You're trying so hard to convince me that he's appealing, gentle, generous... it's as if you yourself don't believe it, not one bit! And you keep saying how nice he is. Really, you don't fall in love with a guy because he's nice!"

And yet if he calls, I'll say "yes." I'll accept his invitation to eat at a restaurant or maybe we'll go to a movie. And when he takes my hand, I won't pull it away.

First conclusion: contrary to what I would like to believe, I don't want to be alone. It's pure selfishness, of course, but I need to feel loved, and right now, this need is stronger than the need to fall in love.

Second conclusion: Without realizing it, I'm more honest with Samira than I am with myself. I keep telling myself that the point of this diary is to see myself more clearly, to better understand my choices, decisions and contradictions. But in reality, it's only a veil I use to cover my eyes. I let my dreams and memories mislead me, certain that my conscious mind — being intact and lucid — will be a more reliable guide than my emotions, to which I resolutely remain blind.

Jerusalem, December 10, 2008
Avner rarely talks politics. But tonight, I don't know, he must have read an article that bothered him, or maybe he just wanted to see what I think, to learn "what camp" I'm in. He started by asking me about Obama's election and his policy on Israel. I told him that it was probably too early to judge but that I believe a distancing of the American administration would take future peace talks down a safer path.

Avner looked at me, scandalized. "If the U.S. cuts its ties to Israel, it's the end of everything! You'd have to be completely unaware or ignorant of reality not to see it! With the threat of Iran, Hezbollah and Hamas, what could Israel do? We'd have no choice: we'd have to take the necessary measures, face all our enemies alone." He lost his temper, but I had trouble believing in his anger. He was mechanically repeating arguments I've heard many times since coming to Israel: "Peace, peace! The only word Obama and the Democrats can pronounce! I want peace, too, just like everyone else in Israel. But the Arabs? Is that what they really want? They tell us we have to negotiate. Okay, I'd like to, but with whom? Hamas? Easy for them to say, those liberal do-gooders, asking us to negotiate with the enemy; they're not the ones with their back to the sea, they're not the ones who were told, 'We're going to wipe you off the map!'"

I would have liked to answer him, to try to lead him away from all those clichés, which he was reeling off like a lesson mindlessly memorized. But what would be the point? He would have thought me naïve or worse yet, condescending. Avner believes that I suffer from the Jews-in-the-Diaspora syndrome: full of good intentions but unable to grasp the complexity of the situation, the dilemmas and impasses that Israelis face on a daily basis.

By saying nothing, by not revealing the other half of what I am, I am lying to both of us. And this excuse – that he wouldn't understand, that he couldn't accept me as I am – is nothing but a red herring. If I had more integrity, I'd break up with him right now.

❄

Jerusalem, December 12, 2008
What I know about Avner:

He is full of thoughtful gestures. Every time we see each other, he brings a little gift: chocolate truffles, a coral necklace, a fountain pen. The other night, he walked back to Mount Scopus with me and when he noticed that I was cold, he took off his jacket and draped it over my shoulders.

He adores insurance. For hours on end, he explains in great detail the pros and cons of various financial products. With this one, I avoid paying withholding tax; that one doesn't pay much at first, but if you let it collect interest, you get good long-term benefits. I make a colossal effort not to seem bored.

He dreams of having a family. A wife too, of course, but a family first and foremost. He has it all planned out: three children, preferably two boys and a girl. He even knows their names: Shlomo, Amiel and Osnat.

He doesn't like it when other men talk to me or even look at me. The other day, we were having iced tea on Dizengoff and the waiter, a husky, well-muscled young man with a big smile, lingered to exchange a bit of meaningless chatter. He had family in Montreal,

spoke a little French and was a student at Tel Aviv University.
While this was going on, Avner pretended he wasn't listening and
nonchalantly consulted his BlackBerry to hide his embarrassment.
When the waiter left, he gave me a dirty look and said, "That waiter
is such a jerk, don't you think?"

He keeps kosher and goes to synagogue every Saturday morning.
He doesn't like Samira.

ABRAHAM IS STANDING. Hands on his face, he listens.

He is waiting for the voice, born of silence, which names him and calls to him: "Abraham!"

Soon he is flooded with the words.

His solitude is inundated with voices. They intertwine and multiply, births that tear him from the world, clouds that obscure his sight.

Which voice belongs to the One? Which voice is not his own?

"Abraham!"

"I am here!"

Like a blind man, under the assault of a thousand whispers, he gropes and loses his way.

"My Lord, is it truly your voice that I hear?"

And the only response is, again, silence.

With hands clenched against his face, Abraham searches within himself for the compelling words that had once seemed so clear and alive: "I will be your promise. You will be, in this world, my presence."

But these words that echo in the depths of his soul are forever extinguished. Abraham tries to follow their meanderings and struggles to rediscover the immense light to which they once blinded him.

To no avail. He heard only sounds, the musicless rhythm of a forgotten encounter.

"Words, words, more words – will you give me nothing else? I gave up everything for you. I left the land where I was born. I renounced man and his beliefs – but you! What sign have you given me that you exist?

"For you, Holy One, I sacrificed my father's idols, those ridiculous little gods – but at least I could touch them and see them.

"You, what is your existence outside of me? Your life, did I not dream it? Your countenance, did I not draw it on the heavens? And your silence that burns my body, your silence that howls out my defeat, is it not the power of the world, the only truth that I have left?"

3

Jerusalem, December 14, 2008
It was sheer stupidity. I don't know why I let myself be persuaded.
Earlier, when I woke up and saw him asleep beside me, I panicked.
I had only one thought in mind: "He has to leave; I have to find a
way to get him out of here."

I have only a vague memory of last night. We'd spent the
afternoon at the beach near Tel Aviv. He'd brought a Frisbee and
wanted to teach me how to play. We ran up and down the wet
sand. Especially him, because despite his instructions, I had
trouble controlling the thing. Sometimes I threw it in the wrong
direction and it would land 10 metres from Avner, and sometimes
I threw it too hard and the Frisbee sailed toward the sea. Without
a word of reproach, Avner ran after it and kindly called out to me
in a booming voice, "Don't worry, it's the wind. There's too much
wind today."

When we got back to Jerusalem, we went to meet Avner's friends
at a Mexican restaurant. The man, whom I already knew, was called
Nathan. He and Avner had done their military service together. He
shook my hand vigorously, and his engaging and dogged smile
displayed an almost professional candour, as if I were a new client
with whom he was sure he'd soon sign a good deal. The name of the
young woman with him was Ronit but she went by Lola, which is her
grandmother's name. She was small and slender but she held herself
very erect, gave me an imposingly haughty stare and tried to look
down at me as if she were a good head taller. Knowing that Hebrew
is not my mother tongue, she spoke to me very slowly and carefully
pronounced each syllable. Then to be sure I was getting the gist, she
repeated the same sentence in English. Several times, I was tempted

to play the fool and make her think I hadn't understood at all, but out of respect for Avner, I restrained myself.

It took a long time for our order to come, and on a signal from Avner, the waiter brought us one margarita after the other to help tide us over. I was only working on my second drink, but I already felt light-headed. I didn't dare stand up to go to the ladies' room; I was too afraid that I'd stumble and fall before I got there. Discouraged, Lola had thrown in the towel. She had finally realized that she had nothing to gain from me and had stopped telling me about her interior design classes and the price of real estate in Tel Aviv. To hide her displeasure, she had turned toward the two men and listened wide-eyed to their conversation, which consisted of sharing their memories of the army. I had already heard these stories often enough – the time they had stolen a young officer's canteen and replaced the water with vodka, the one where their captain had caught them using their flashlights to illuminate a late-night poker game, and the one where Nathan, having suffered a leg injury, had spent a month in hospital under the care of a voluptuous Russian nurse. Every once in a while Lola interrupted, commented on their adventures and shared her own. To evoke their laughter or surprise, she embellished them a bit, and the men reacted courteously, sometimes erupting in laughter, sometimes looking shocked.

The combined effect of the margaritas and Lola's baffling tales had tired me out and I wanted only one thing: for Avner to finally take me home. As we left the restaurant, Lola and Nathan went in one direction and I instantly felt relieved. Perhaps it was only in comparison to the other couple's oppressive presence, but finding myself alone with Avner again seemed like a sweet reward, as if I had dreamed of nothing else the entire evening.

For some absurd reason, I wanted to show Avner my appreciation, so I gave him my arm. He must have seen this as a sign of affection and he immediately put his arm around my shoulders. I think that moment marked the tipping point. I'd had too much to drink and for the first time since my arrival in Jerusalem, I had stopped worrying about myself.

The landscape around me had changed. In the still-lively streets, coloured by the revelers' laughter and the harsh neon lights, it was no longer Avner walking at my side but an imaginary person, a man with potential, the one whose shadow accompanied me when, as a teenager, I no longer knew what the future would hold.

We walked in silence and I already knew that I would say yes. When we got to my building, he didn't even stop to kiss me, as he usually did. He simply pushed open the door and followed me inside. With a ceremonious gesture, he opened the elevator and invited me to enter, slightly tilting his head forward like an elevator operator in a big department store. I smiled politely at him. I felt him staring at me, examining me, guessing at the skin beneath my blouse. Even now, I don't understand what was going on inside me. Was it desire? Fear? The simple need to give in, to let this man decide, in the improbable hope that he would change, that he would prove to be this fabulous, impossible being that had deserted my imagination so long ago?

When I opened the door to my room, it seemed as if I were betraying someone or breaking a taboo. We sat on my bed and he put his hand on my knee. I kept my eyes lowered, like a child about to be reprimanded. Then, putting his curled forefinger under my chin, he raised my head and leaned toward me so that our faces met. His two eyebrows forming a peak above his nose and his hesitant smile gave him an imploring, pained expression, as if he were burdened by the knowledge that I wasn't fully present. A few beads of sweat collected along his temples and made their way down between the tufts of his thinning hair. I was thinking to myself, "His age and already going bald." And I felt badly for him. Was it this awakening of pity that kept me from rejecting him?

Sitting at my desk now, I watch him sleeping. He has no clue. I think he's even smiling in his sleep. He's reliving his conquest; his chubby hands that pin me to the bed; my body, that pale, frail thing that he finally possesses; his pleasure, of course, and the blissful, blind *certainty that I came with him. He's happy with himself. When he wakes up, he'll call my name, put his moist lips on my shoulder and ask me to make him some coffee. In the afternoon, he'll pick me up at school and in the evening, we'll go out to eat. Then he'll take me to his place and last night will begin all over again.*

No. Impossible. I have to put a stop to this now, before it goes any further. I made an error in judgement. It has nothing to do with him… I'm the one who's at fault. I like him a lot but that's all. I was wrong. I don't know what came over me. I'd had too much to drink, maybe, and I was feeling alone. I needed to be held or he'd aroused my emotions. It doesn't matter. What counts is that this cannot go on any longer.

❊

From: Daniel
To: Sara
Subject: News from Montreal
Monday, December 15, 2008, 8:34 p.m.

Dear Sara,
I was so happy to talk to you yesterday. I've been a bit worried. I'm slowly getting used to the crutches. Everyone in the department is suddenly very nice to me. They smile and ask me what happened and hurry to open doors for me… Even Manon, the secretary, seems to have softened. She usually has some reason to reproach me (I didn't properly fill out a form, I was late for the last meeting, etc.). Anyway, can you believe she offered me a box of chocolates?! I can't get over it!
I've been invited to give a lecture on Rembrandt at Columbia University in March. I think I'll accept.
It snowed again today. I miss you.
Papa

＊

Jerusalem, December 15, 2008
I don't have the heart to talk to Avner. He sent me several texts during
the day. I only glanced at them: "I'm thinking of you…", "…your
smell…", "…a surprise tonight." This morning, when he woke up, I
was ready to leave to go to class. I let him kiss me and asked him to
make sure he closed the door properly behind him. "See you tonight!"
He said these words and I suddenly realized the depth of the chasm
that separates us. To Avner, there's nothing more to say. We are a
couple and tonight, like all couples, we'll meet up, we'll go out, we'll
eat supper together. But I don't want to be a "we." I don't see myself
with him and I don't want him to be part of my life.

When he called tonight, I didn't answer. I just sent him a text to
make my excuses: I have a stomach virus and am staying in bed to rest.

＊

Daniel paid the bill. Samira waited for him outside. The waitress
approached the table and bent down to pick something up off the
floor: Samira's sunglasses. She gave them to Daniel and asked, "Are
these your daughter's?" Speechless, he looked at the waitress. He
took the glasses without making the effort to correct her mistake.

At first, the waitress's error had touched him: she hadn't thought
him the kind of man who would have a relationship with a woman
half his age. But soon, this innocent vanity gave way to a biting pain:
no, Samira was not his daughter. Of his own daughter, there had
been no news. She had disappeared. Eighteen days ago now.

Outside, the rays of the setting sun enveloped the passersby in a
blinding light. Sara put on the sunglasses. Large and round, like a
bee's eyes, they covered half her face.

"You should cover your head," Daniel told her. "It's still very hot."

To avoid contradicting him, she took a blue-and-white-striped
cap out of her bag and put it on her head, at a jaunty angle.

"There, now I look like a real tourist!"

They walked through Yemin Moshe to the Jaffa Gate, then entered the Armenian Quarter.

"Do you know this guy Ibrahim?"

"Not very well," Samira replied, raising her sunglasses. "I met him a few times. Sara talked a lot about him lately. She was... she was very much in love, you know."

"I don't understand why she never told me about him."

"She was waiting for you to come visit her. She wanted you to meet him without having any preconceived notions. I have to say... he's kind of a strange guy. He rarely looks you in the eye; he seems a little bit lost, as if he's just landed and is waiting for instructions. It's not just that he stutters, but when he talks to you, you feel like he's talking to himself or that he's reciting a monologue in a play."

"Where's he from? Jerusalem?"

"Nazareth, I think. At least that's where his parents live."

"Is he studying archaeology, too?"

"No, he and Sara had only one class together. He studies literature. His thesis is on David Grossman. When they started dating, Sara told me about their conversations. It seemed awfully intense to me. He has some bizarre theories... About God, about religion..."

"Meaning?"

"Well, for example, he told Sara that he's not an atheist, not an agnostic, not a believer in the true sense of the word, but that he's 'post-atheist.' In other words, after having lost faith and rejected religion in all its dimensions, he's now trying to come back to it, to reintegrate the practice into his life, with sincerity but without blind devotion. In any case, that's what I understood from Sara's explanations. They have these passionate discussions about the Koran, biblical characters, their relationship with God. But I always reacted to Sara's enthusiasm with some skepticism – it's in my nature, after all – and soon she stopped talking to me about him."

Daniel was imagining Sara and Ibrahim, lying side by side, staring at the ceiling, late at night. Surely Sara tells him about her mother, her illness, her death and the crisis that followed. She confides in this odd young man and he listens. She tells him her prayers, her certainty that God would cure her mother and the immense sense of betrayal that gripped her after Leila died.

Daniel had not followed Sara in her prayers. He'd never felt this need. He had his own anguish to manage. He could never let it overwhelm him; Sara still needed him. So he threw himself into his painting because that was all he knew how to do. He, who had only ever painted portraits, began to paint landscapes, cities, industrial structures in a state of neglect, scenes of ruin and violence. In this way he was sure that Leila's features, her face, her hands, would not return as the result of a too-ardent brush stroke surreptitiously inserting itself into his painting.

Now, he told himself, Sara has perhaps found someone in whom she can confide, to whom she can explain the emptiness and the loss of God. Perhaps at this precise moment, they are together; perhaps they've shut themselves away from the world and are only waiting for a sign before coming back to civilization and reconnecting with their loved ones.

❄

Jerusalem, December 16, 2008
There, it's done. I can finally breathe.

Yesterday, Avner came to pick me up at the university. He suggested taking me home to meet his parents. I politely refused, pretending that I still didn't feel completely well. So we ended up in an Italian restaurant in Nahalat Shiva.

As I listened to him tell about his day, I thought about what I was going to tell him later. I had to find the right words. I couldn't hesitate or hurt him unnecessarily, but most importantly, I could leave no room for doubt. None of this "I think maybe we should stop seeing each other for a while, I think we should take some time to think…" No, I had to avoid all ambiguity; otherwise I would never extricate myself.

As I stared ahead at the stucco walls decorated with frescoes of a pink-and-blue landscape, I felt him looking at me. No admiration, no tenderness, not even desire. His expression showed only that I belonged to him, that his quest had come to an end and that this banal dream of his – a respectable family living a well-ordered life, at the top of which sits enthroned an obedient and fertile woman – could finally become a reality. Maybe I'm exaggerating a little, but that's the image I kept in mind so that I could break up with him.

As soon as I opened my mouth, he understood. His face, which had been so animated in anticipation of the evening's pleasures, suddenly shrank; the brows furrowed and his mouth resumed its usual bitter pout.

For once, I didn't struggle to find my words. My little speech had been well-prepared. "Everything happened too fast. It has nothing to do with you. I don't really know what I want, I'm not ready" and so on. He insisted a bit: "I don't get it, I thought we were good together." In his head, he must have had all kind of plans, a shared life, and it was this future that had been stolen from him in one fell swoop. When he asked me if there was someone else, I didn't want to lie. I repeated that he was above reproach and that it was all my fault, that I was the one who'd led us to this impasse.

Realizing that I wasn't going to change my mind, whatever my reasons for ending it had been, Avner asked for the bill and got up to leave. He avoided my eyes, as if I were no longer there. And that's when I spoke that terrible little sentence, that cowardly, irrevocable phrase that vanquishes dreams and even invalidates the past: "You know, I'd like to stay friends." He acted as if he hadn't heard and we got into his car.

He didn't call today. I checked my phone all day, afraid that he might have sent a text. But thank goodness, there was nothing.

I finally feel relieved but not yet completely free. I still feel his presence; it sticks to my skin, not like a weight or a bad memory, but like a threat whose shape you can scarcely imagine.

Jerusalem, December 17, 2008

I didn't actually write down everything that happened. Avner didn't start crying, that's true; he didn't show his pain. We avoided the melodramatic. But on the way home, in his car, I was terrified. I had barely closed the car door when he stomped on the gas pedal. At the first red light, he braked so hard that my forehead almost hit the dashboard. I turned toward him. His eyes were riveted to the stop light, his lips taut, his hands clenching the steering wheel.

Slowly, without looking at me, Avner leaned over to the glove compartment, took out a CD and put it into the CD player. The car windows began to vibrate furiously: it was a conga solo, a hellish salsa loud enough to wake the dead. Unperturbed, Avner peeled out, making the tires squeal on the damp pavement. With one foot on the accelerator and the other on the brake, he honked feverishly, terrorizing pedestrians and eliciting frightened looks at every corner. At red lights, he impatiently revved the engine. The frenzy of the music seemed to dictate his movements, and when he sped up to pass a car, it was to the furious rhythm of Poncho Sanchez's drums.

I don't know what came over him. Was it the frustration of having accepted our separation without an argument? Was he suddenly mad at himself for not having defended himself, for not having tried to hold onto me? Or was he just trying to scare me? Maybe he wanted to prove to me that for a brief moment he was master of my life and that, if I escaped unharmed, it was thanks only to his magnanimity.

Despite my repeated pleas, Avner refused to slow down on the road leading to the dorm on Mount Scopus. Instead, he let the car skid around the tight turns and, like a fugitive certain that he would be caught but continuing his mad flight with perverse determination, he seethed with anger, pressing erratically on the gas and passing dangerously close to the cars approaching from the other direction. I didn't dare look at the road. I thought only of the moment when I would at last be home, when I could get out of that damn car (just five more minutes, just four… c'mon, you have to keep it together).

Finally, with one last slamming of the brakes and one last jolt, we made it back to my dorm. I jumped out of the car, leaving the plastic bag with the CDs and the scarf he had loaned me on the back seat. I didn't turn around to check, but I felt his eyes following me. A deadly stare, capable of anything.

❋

Thanks to Professor Oren, Daniel had the phone number of Sara's friend Tamar. "I'm not supposed to do this sort of thing, but given the circumstances…" In a hesitant voice, Oren had capitulated.

When he called, Tamar proved to be gracious. Her voice was marked by concern and a sincere sympathy but free of pity. She insisted that Daniel visit her at home.

In the building's stairwell, Daniel was besieged by the smell of fresh paint, which for a brief moment transported him into the distant past, to the first day of school when he and Sara had walked down the corridors that had, as if by some miracle, become white again over the summer.

The young woman opened the door and led him into a dusty living room furnished with a coffee table and sofas covered with grey sheets. The floor was strewn with cardboard boxes.

"Thank you for seeing me," Daniel hastened to say. "I'm sure you're very busy… with your moving?"

"Please, it's no problem," Tamar replied in a warm voice.

She asked Daniel to sit down, slipped into the kitchen and soon returned, carrying a tray with a silver teapot and two cups.

"So you met Sara at Khirbet Qeiyafa, right?"

"Yes," she answered. "Sara and I were on the same team during the dig. She really loved the place and was eager to go back, I think."

"Do you see each other a lot?"

"Yes, especially since Gaza. When the attacks happened, in January, I took her to a demonstration. And we often eat together or with a group of friends. I think it was hard for her... this double identity. She was often at odds with... But when it was just the two of us, she felt more comfortable. She often talked about her mother – and about you, too," she added with a smile.

"Didn't she seem worried to you lately?" Daniel asked.

"Yes, more than worried. She was afraid... You know about her relationship with Avner?"

"Yes, she told me about him. I went to meet him a few days ago—"

"What did you think of him?"

"He seemed fairly likeable. But I understand he didn't take their break-up very well."

"Yes, you could say that. He wouldn't stop calling her, harassing her... I offered to talk to Avner but she said no. She was afraid it would only make matters worse. But the last time we saw each other, something else seemed to be bothering her. She told me about a cousin of Ibrahim's, a guy named Tareq."

"Did he want to hurt her?"

"No, not her – I don't think she'd even met him. But it seems he has something against Ibrahim. Some kind of rivalry... I didn't quite understand and since she seemed hesitant, I didn't want to ask too many questions."

"Do you think she and Ibrahim might have been afraid and could have left together?"

"It's possible. Since her disappearance, I've sometimes wondered... But then, no, it's not terribly likely..."

"What do you mean?"

"I don't know... I thought that if she'd wanted to get away, find some safe haven, she might have gone back to the site at Khirbet Qeiyafa..."

❋

From: Daniel
To: Sara
Subject: A good movie
Friday, December 19, 2008, 11:14 p.m.

Dear Sara,

The term is finally over! Tonight, I rented an Israeli movie, Bonjour Monsieur Shlomi. I thought of you. It's the story of a 16-year-old boy who dedicates himself to everyone around him – his wheel-chair-bound grandfather, his mother (an unpleasant woman), his sisters' twins... he forgets about himself in all his devotion, until he meets Rona, the neighbourhood gardener. It was a bit wacky, a bit romantic – I think you would have liked it.

By the way, you haven't said anything more about that boy Avner... I send you a big hug,

Papa

From: Sara
To: Daniel
Subject: A good movie
Saturday, December 20, 2008, 8:02 a.m.

Good morning, Papa.

Thanks for your email, now I want to see that movie.

Actually it didn't work out with Avner. I'll explain on the phone.

Kisses,

Sara

❄

Jerusalem, December 22, 2008
A few days ago, I started studying again. I'm reading like mad. My
paper on the dig at Khirbet Qeiyafa is going well (even though,

obviously, we didn't find any trace of the famous battle between David and Goliath). In the evening, Samira and I go out to supper, alone or with friends. I feel as if I've found my life again, right where I left it. From time to time, I'll hear some salsa music or walk by a man in the street who is wearing the same aftershave, and the memory of Avner briefly crosses my mind. But I don't dwell on it.

Jerusalem, December 23, 2008
I went to the movie theatre to see Woody Allen's Deconstructing Harry *again. There are some very funny scenes but the ending is full of wisdom – a wry, somewhat sardonic wisdom: "All people know the same truth. Our lives consist of how we choose to distort it."*

Jerusalem, December 26, 2008
I had dinner with Dov and Tamar tonight. Instead of going to a restaurant, they invited me to their place. They just moved in together, on the 11th floor of a building in the French Hill neighbourhood. Tamar immediately started apologizing: they hadn't had time to unpack all the boxes or to clean everything ("You should have seen the state the previous tenants left the apartment in!"). As he served me a drink, Dov gently contradicted Tamar. "It wasn't all that dirty. The truth is that you have such high standards that even Buckingham Palace wouldn't be clean enough for you!" Tamar simply smiled at him and led me by the arm to complete the "palace tour."

Their bedroom opens onto a balcony that Tamar had already decorated with flowers. In the distance, we could see the cypresses on Mount Scopus. The bathroom was full of sunlight. "We haven't had time to put up blinds, so at night, we shower in the dark," Tamar explained. We walked down a narrow hallway whose walls still smelled of fresh paint. Then we entered the kitchen, a narrow room littered with brooms, floor cloths and disinfectant wipes.

Back in the living room, Dov was setting the table. Tamar walked over to him and, without reproach, discreetly corrected his mistakes: on the right, the knife with its cutting edge facing the plate, the spoon and the dessert fork properly aligned, the wine glass slightly to the right of the water glass.

I looked at the boxes still filled with knickknacks stacked up against the dining room wall, the piles of dusty books and the scattered clothing. Despite the mess, the place had a strange feeling of permanence, order and an impenetrable intimacy. In each look that Dov and Tamar exchanged, you could almost hear the echo of their two confident voices: "Twenty years from now, we'll still be here." Despite the difficulties, inevitable disappointments, hard blows, pauses and setbacks, each will find in the other the promised foundation, the welcoming doorstep. From now on, their life will be governed by the fact that they are a couple.

I am happy for them, especially for Tamar, who is so kind to me. I'm not jealous — well, yes, maybe a bit. Because I sometimes feel lost and because I don't know if I will ever be able to find such certainty.

❄

From: Daniel
To: Sara
Subject: Montreal under the snow
Saturday, December 27, 2008, 3:31 p.m.

Dear Sara,
I was sorry to hear that it didn't work out with Avner. But from the little you told me on the phone, it seems to me that it's better this way. If you're not in love, you shouldn't force it.
Yesterday, another storm. I holed up in the apartment and spent the day marking papers.
Tomorrow, I leave for Sainte-Marguerite. The Boiverts invited me to their chalet for a few days. We'll celebrate New Year's Eve together. If you want, you can reach me on my cell.
Warm hugs,
Papa

✳

Worry, vast and suffocating, stayed with Daniel, dictating every one of his movements and guiding every thought. But the anguish that had initially maintained a tyrannical embargo on any sort of joy was, by force of habit, allowing little pleasures to slip in at last – a walk through the silent streets of Jerusalem at dawn, a spinach salad at noon, and to help him fall asleep late at night, a random American adventure film that was unlikely to stir up memories. Sometimes Daniel would exchange meaningless pleasantries with the hotel concierge or the waitress who brought him his daily orange juice. Sometimes even a smile from Samira or a hand laid on his shoulder gave his racing mind a brief reprieve through which he gained the sense of a world where everything had returned to normal.

Routine didn't extinguish the fear, but it provided signposts that, one by one, helped Daniel move through the day. First, the call to Detective Ben-Ami. Daniel reviewed the situation, told the policeman what he'd learned: that Sara had felt threatened, that Avner had kept calling her, contrary to what he'd told Daniel, and that she'd been receiving anonymous phone calls late at night. Ben-Ami scrupulously took notes, even though he implied that he was already aware of it all. Next, breakfast at the hotel restaurant or at the Starbucks on the corner, followed by a long walk, usually in the Armenian Quarter. It wasn't until afternoon that his anxiety resurfaced and new scenarios piled up in his head. The most optimistic first: Sara had slipped away with Ibrahim. Madly in love, they had decided to take a vacation without telling anyone. Who knew? Maybe they had even gone abroad, to Cyprus or Morocco. But questions gradually eroded this reassuring hypothesis: why didn't she at least call? Why wasn't she answering her phone? Why hadn't she told anyone? Then Daniel had to allow the sobering thoughts to return. Had Sara and Ibrahim felt threatened? By whom? Had they tried to run away? Had they been kidnapped? Attacked? The words slowly gave way to images. A series of violent scenes furiously unfolded in his head.

They harassed and pursued him. And his panic-stricken mind fled vainly from one to the next, like a hunted fox that escapes the first dog only to throw itself between the teeth of the second.

In the evening, after her classes, Samira called Daniel to exchange their news. Daniel told her of his last conversation with Ben-Ami, described his doubts and theories. Sometimes, she came to see him at his hotel and they had coffee together. Daniel also asked her about herself, her schoolwork and her family. At first, he was only trying to be polite, but when she confided her uncertainties or mentioned her tense relationship with her father, Daniel tried to advise her as he would have done with Sara. And in the regular rhythm that now organized his day and his fear, Samira's voice in the evening became a welcome break, anticipated with impatience, even though he knew she would bring only momentary relief.

❈

Jerusalem, December 28, 2008
Gaza was bombed yesterday. Here, at the university, that's all they talk about. Samira's in a state of shock. Usually so talkative, she's taken refuge in silence. She's choking on her anger. When I ask a question, she answers only by nodding or shaking her head. She brings her knees up to her chest, wraps her arms around them and hides her face in the little hollow that they form. I assume that she's crying, but her expression is probably frozen, impenetrable, devoid of all feeling.

Jerusalem, January 6, 2009
At the end of his course on the Judeo-Roman wars, Yehuda Sofrim spoke to us about the "heroes of Masada." Their collective suicide, he explained in a solemn tone that was suddenly full of emotion, conveys lessons that cannot leave us unmoved. The besieged at Masada accepted the ultimate sacrifice. They acted not out of cowardice but, paradoxically, for the survival of the Jewish people. Their example has

96

been a source of inspiration throughout the ages, and in light of the new dangers threatening Israel, it is more relevant than ever. Because to this day, the Jewish people have been isolated; to this day, its enemies yearn for its destruction; to this day, it must face, alone, the criticism and the hatred.

Coming from Sofrim, this little speech was surprising. First of all, because all that matters in his class are the facts; he is not concerned with their interpretation or with the analysis of "broad trends." Also, because he's not in the habit of sharing his political opinions with us. On the contrary, he tries to expunge all references to current events from his lectures, happy to share in great detail the dates, the armies present, the battle sites and the number of dead.

What drove him today to so openly reveal his feelings, to so clearly take sides? This war is having a strange effect: those who were already critical of the Israeli authorities find one more justification for their hostility and give free rein to their recriminations, and those who defend the government even while acknowledging its faults now do not hesitate to subscribe to the militaristic discourse and dare not express an opinion that might appear contradictory. As Samira says, it's not just Gaza getting bombed, it's the centre, the moderates, those who still believe in a just peace.

And where am I in all this? I feel only anger and shame. Ashamed that I've accepted my impotence in the face of this war that isn't one. Ashamed of my silence (but isn't it worse to get riled up, to condemn, to vilify when we know that our words won't change anything?). Ashamed of not taking a side and continuing to vacillate. Ashamed that I don't see myself in the suffering of the Gazans, ashamed of my good Muslim conscience, a victim by proxy, heir to an offense that I did not suffer. Ashamed also of feeling Jewish but not Israeli, ashamed that I don't experience as a threat the opprobrium heaped on this country.

Jerusalem, January 8, 2009

I finally decided to go to the demonstration with Tamar. There were 10 of us and in the bus that took us to Tel Aviv, we talked in small groups, two by two, in muted voices, like a band of thieves planning their next heist. We joined an eclectic and noisy crowd on Dizengoff Street, at the point where the march was supposed to start. Sleepy-eyed students brandished signs bearing slogans written with black felt-tip pen whose ink was already being erased by the light rain that was falling: "No to war!" and "Immediate ceasefire!" Among the students, a few guys in their forties, hands in their pockets, looked worriedly from right to left, searching in vain to locate the leaders who would give the signal to depart. One of them, a man with an emaciated face, a greying beard and a T-shirt bearing the washed-out image of Che Guevara, was taking pictures with his cell phone. Another was standing near a low wall, calmly eating his breakfast.

Like these aging leftists, I also tried to appear composed. I watched the others, standing on tiptoe as I pretended to look for someone. A stocky young man, already potbellied and wearing round glasses too small for his chubby face, walked from group to group, distributing signs and leaflets. I tried to smile at him, but he walked by me as if he hadn't seen me. A few minutes later, Tamar came toward me to introduce me to her friends, but after the first greetings and a few forced smiles, they resumed their conversation without another thought to my presence. I felt a great chasm between myself and all these well-meaning demonstrators.

The group got underway; a long gaily coloured line snaked through the streets of Tel Aviv. I did as the others did: I held up my sign, I signed the petitions that were circulating, I shouted the slogans chanted by the troop's leader until I was hoarse. Around noon, we reached the Kirya – the headquarters of the Ministry of Defense. There we waited not for the government's representatives but for a group of counterdemonstrators who were scandalized by Israelis who dared to challenge the army's actions. There were lively exchanges

("Go back home! You should be ashamed! Don't you have anything better to do than attack the nation that defends your rights? You're nothing but a bunch of traitors!" and then, "We have the right to be heard! You are the traitors! We're the conscience of this country!"), followed quickly by insults, then scuffles and finally fistfights. Punches were thrown on the front line while to the rear, all kinds of projectiles, signs, water bottles and beer cans were thrown at the opposition. I left just as the police came to disperse the combatants. I was lucky and escaped with only a bruise on my arm. When Tamar called me a few hours later to invite me to join her for coffee with a group of friends with whom she'd taken shelter, I declined, saying I was too tired.

I returned to my room as if I were coming out of a dream. Yes, I had participated, but I hadn't been fully present. I had accompanied a group whose ideas I felt I shared. I had yelled along with the others but I hadn't felt their anger or their passion or their immense certainty. Why had I followed Tamar and her friends? Just so that I could tell myself that I'm not indifferent? That I, too, am able to act? But can a clear conscience really be so easily bought?

I won't watch the news tonight. I don't want to hear the analysts holding forth on this insignificant minority of clueless, ungrateful "traitors" who are putting the nation's security at risk. Traitor. And what if they were right? What if I'm just a traitor? But for that to be true, I'd have to feel a little bit Jewish. Yet there, in the brawl at the Kirya, under the hail of bottles and empty cans that the assailants were throwing in our faces, I wasn't on the demonstrators' side. I was an intruder, a Muslim girl lost among all those activists who wanted only her well-being, lost because she understood nothing of that hate, because she didn't know anymore, because she didn't want to know where justice lay and who was right.

✢

From: Daniel
To: Sara
Subject: Demonstration in Tel Aviv
Friday, January 9, 2009, 8:40 p.m.

Dear Sara,

Yesterday I went to the hospital to get my cast off. What a relief!
I hope you're alright. Yesterday I saw a report from Tel Aviv about a demonstration against the war with Gaza. Things degenerated quickly and there were injuries. They said that several students from Hebrew U took part in it. I hope you weren't there. Take good care of yourself.

Your loving father

From: Sara
To: Daniel
Subject: Demonstration in Tel Aviv
Saturday, January 10, 2009, 7:24 a.m.

Hi, Papa.

I did in fact hear about that demonstration.

Rest assured, I stayed warm and cozy in my room. I have a lot of reading to do for my thesis so I don't go out much.

The atmosphere at the university is very tense. Opinions are divided. In one camp are those who demand an end to the offensive. In the other, those who support the army and denounce the critics.

I can't wait for this so-called war to be over.

I'll call you tomorrow.

Sara

❄

Jerusalem, January 12, 2009

Conversation with Papa last night. I didn't tell him I'd participated in the demonstration. He would have worried and bombarded me with questions. What would that have accomplished? He's far away, he's afraid, it's better to protect him.

Jerusalem, January 15, 2009

It's always the stranger inside me who wins. When I'm with Samira and her family, I feel more Jewish than ever. I understand their jokes, share their concerns and am shocked by the same injustices. But I don't see myself in them. That, it seems to me, would be too easy. That would mean behaving like an imposter, exercising rights that are not mine, mistakenly believing myself to be united with the others in their faith in a common destiny.

It's the same with Tamar, Dov and their friends. They treat me as one of their own and I, for my part, play the game as best I know how. But there's a great silence within me and my perspective on life comes from somewhere elsewhere. They talk about Arabs: "they" are being betrayed by their elite, the majority of "them" want peace, "they" have the same dreams and ambitions as we do… Listening to them, I can't help but think that "they" means me.

Sometimes I envy them. Samira, Tamar and Avner have attachments; they feel history moving through them, they know the ways of the world. And most of all, they're not alone. The others aren't just "the others." They are friends, relatives, fellow travellers.

I cannot and never will be able to say "we."

Jerusalem, January 28, 2009

The Israeli army pulled out of Gaza a week ago. In both camps they count the dead. Now the talk is of an investigation, war crimes and legal proceedings.

ON HIS KNEES, his back curved down toward the ground, Abraham breathes heavily.

With fingers curled against his fevered temples, he weeps in anger:

"Where is the sign, the infallible proof that you are not me? Permit me, my Lord, to feel your presence. In the sky, write your name, which echoes within me. Use your voice to make blind nature tremble. Draw your face on the bare flank of the mountain.

"When you turn away from me, I hear only the mockery of men: 'Abraham. You're nothing but a dreamer. And your God, this so-called soul of all the living, is nothing but one of your foolish dreams.'

"How can I answer them? Where is the immense wave that will break over them? Where is the fire that will erase their memory for all time?

"I have nothing but my word – and yours, which has never broken free from my heart.

"Can you not, just once, come forth from my solitude?

"Will I ever know if your breath, which I feel roaring within me, is that of another life? If I die, will you survive me?"

Exhausted and distraught, Abraham dashes down the mountain. He falls several times and gets up. His face and arms are scraped raw and his hands are bloodied.

Eyes fixed on the mist that envelops Mount Moriah, he turns back one last time and murmurs as if he were now speaking only to himself: "My God, return to me! My solitude has filled this world, and this world is empty, such was the extent of my desire to find you in it.

"I will be nearer to you in death, because at least then my absence will be equal to yours."

Abraham remains standing for a long time, his look lost in the distance, far beyond the mountain.

"But before I die, I must know if indeed everything is possible in this world."

And on the long road back, these last words accompany him and dictate his footsteps, like a final judgement, sole light within the silence.

4

Jerusalem, February 4, 2009

*That's the third time. The other day, when I saw him approaching
with the saltshaker, I was rather intrigued. I was at the university
café. I had just sat down to eat my daily plate of French fries, and
since there was no salt on my table, I stood up and scanned the
cafeteria, looking for a saltshaker. He must have watched me and
guessed what I was doing. Without giving me a chance to leave my
table, he came toward me cradling an object in the palm of his hand
as if it were a delicate crystal sculpture. With his long beard, thick
glasses and shabby felt hat, he made me think of an orthodox Jew. I
noticed his eyes in particular: an intense blue, liquid and vibrant,
that contrasted sharply with his black hair. From this frosty gaze
came a light so raw that it was hard to read its expression. I thanked
him and accepted his offering, and he quickly went back to sit at
his table near the bay window.*

*The day before yesterday, Monday, there was already salt on my
table, but the rabbi was there just the same. This time, instead of
handing me the saltshaker, he furtively placed it on the table and
turned on his heel before I could say a word. Today, the same little
game: he passed close to my table, his head held high, his eyes staring
off into the distance, and with a brush of his hand, he discreetly
placed a saltshaker next to my plate of fries.*

*Tonight, when I told Samira about the incident, she looked at
me with a smile and said, "You know, in this country, we sometimes
meet people who are a little strange. But your weirdo doesn't seem
too dangerous. Next time, you should take the lead and bring him
a saltshaker. Who knows? Maybe he'll decide to talk to you!"*

Jerusalem, February 6, 2009

I took Samira's advice. I didn't take him a saltshaker, but I went up to his table, near the window, where he always eats. He seemed very absorbed in his reading – a book in Hebrew whose title I couldn't see. When he noticed me, he invited me to sit down with a wave of his hand. He didn't say anything; he just sat and smiled at me. Having found the courage to make the first move, I didn't think that I'd also have to make the effort to start the conversation.

But he just watched me. His eyes, which now turned ash-green, were glued to me as if it were my duty to explain myself. To keep the silence from settling in, I finally asked him what he was reading. That's when I understood his reluctance to speak to me: he stutters. With great effort, he managed to answer me: "It's... it's a b-b-book by David G... G... Grossman." And to avoid having to pronounce the title, he showed me the cover: The Smile of the Lamb.

That's when I realized I recognized his face. I knew I'd seen him somewhere, but where? In the university hallways? At the dorm on Mount Scopus? The movie theatre? Finally, I placed him: at the beginning of the year, he had also been in Professor Barnathan's class on biblical archaeology. But he disappeared after the first two sessions. I remember that he sat in the front, by himself, constantly frowning to better see the images projected on the screen. During the breaks, instead of having coffee with the rest of the students, he stayed in his seat with his nose buried in a book, as if he'd been punished.

I didn't dare ask too many questions, considering the energy he had to expend each time he had to answer me. But soon he was the one who insisted on telling me about his reading and his studies. He was crazy about David Grossman, Bialik and Agnon. He tried his best to explain the subject of his thesis, then in desperation, he finally wrote the title on a paper napkin: "The Influence of Bible Stories on Israeli Literature from 1948 to 1967."

I wanted to know more, but I chose not to press him. I had a hard time listening to him stumble over each word, even if he didn't seem too bothered by it. He mentioned Grossman's books, was surprised I hadn't read any and promised to loan me one. I told him that I would prefer to read it in French since I didn't feel I knew Hebrew well enough yet to read novels. He contradicted me, finding my Hebrew excellent – especially the accent, he said, raising his finger as a professor would – and besides, Grossman's language is very simple and pure, and I wouldn't have any trouble adjusting to it.

I'm back in my room and I can't concentrate on my essay. I keep replaying the scenario of our conversation, and I can't help feeling that the most important part escaped me. I feel like I've met a character from a novel, someone not entirely real – someone too bizarre, too eccentric not to have been invented, but too alive to be just a figment of the imagination. We exchanged only a few words, we know almost nothing about each other, and yet I feel I have been laid bare and I almost regret my few insignificant sentences because I feel that they revealed me too completely.

Jerusalem, February 10, 2009
His name is Ibrahim. He was born in Nazareth. He is most certainly not a rabbi.

Why did I assume that he was Jewish? Because of his clothes and unaccented Hebrew? Or because of our chat about his reading and his admiration for David Grossman? I really must be full of prejudices if I think that only a Jew could be passionate about Israeli literature and the author of a thesis on the Bible.

❋

From: Daniel
To: Sara
Subject: Rembrandt
Tuesday, February 10, 2009, 7:28 a.m.

Dear Sara,
I was happy to talk to you yesterday. You seemed less worried.

Last weekend, I continued preparing the text for my lecture. Professor Bomgrich, the one who invited me to Columbia, asked me to talk about my book on Rembrandt and Turner. I find it a bit boring.

After all these years, going back to the subject of my doctorate is a little like explaining old family pictures to a stranger. It's really not what I feel like doing now. And all these theories on "light as a medium for the form" seem too abstract and, frankly, too outdated. Saturday, I'll be in the country. I look forward to your call next Sunday.

Big hug,

Papa

From: Sara

To: Daniel

Subject: Rembrandt

Wednesday, February 11, 2009, 6:45 a.m.

Thanks for your email, Papa. I'm happy to hear you're making progress with your text. Send it to me when you finish, I really want to read it. I'm sure it's not as bad as you would lead me to believe! Kisses,

Sara

❄

Samira looked through Sara's papers and found the address of the Awads, Ibrahim's parents. She talked Daniel into going with her to Nazareth.

It was Ibrahim's mother who came to the door. Daniel let Samira start the conversation. Although he understood Arabic, he rarely spoke it, and Samira was in a better position to gain the woman's trust. First, she apologized for arriving unannounced, then explained the reason for their visit. Mrs. Awad was a woman in her sixties, prematurely wrinkled but with sparkling eyes that must once have harboured ardent dreams. She frowned suspiciously at first but then invited them to come in. They followed her into a dark, humid hallway that led to the living room.

Lined up on shelves over the television were frames of various sizes. Several of the photos showed Ibrahim as a child. A big, unsmiling boy stood next to him. This must have been Tareq. In the courtyard, they could hear hens clucking furiously, as if to protest the arrival of intruders.

"We're sorry to bother you like this," Samira began. "I… we haven't heard from Sara in over two weeks. I know that she and your son were close… Do you think they might be together?"

"I don't know. It's possible." Her voice was gravelly, as if she had done a lot of yelling and had just calmed down.

Samira persisted. "Have you spoken to Ibrahim recently?"

"No. He was supposed to have dinner here two weeks ago and—"

Her voice breaking, she paused. She tried to suppress her anxiety but despite her efforts, her face slowly crumbled and the pain crept in, spreading across her forehead and narrowing her dry lips. Soon enough the dike broke and the woman began to weep.

Initially confused, Samira approached her and put a hand on her arm. "I'm so sorry… I understand your concern. I had an idea… I thought maybe you knew where they might have gone."

Ibrahim's mother raised her head, took a handkerchief from her sleeve to dry her eyes. She regarded Samira with a look that might have appeared warm and understanding, but her mouth quickly curled into a bitter, haughty smile.

"The police asked me the same questions. My husband and I were treated to two visits from the detective himself. He wanted to know about Ibrahim's comings and goings, when we last spoke to him, why he hadn't called, if his behaviour had changed recently… he even asked for pictures of our son, supposedly to help his investigation. But I wasn't fooled; I know perfectly well that he suspects our son of wanting to hurt your daughter," she said, turning toward Daniel. "I wouldn't be surprised if the detective thinks Ibrahim is holding her prisoner somewhere."

"But that's ridiculous. Sara and Ibrahim are totally in love!" Samira replied.

"I know. He even brought her here a few weeks ago. It was in March, I think. He was so proud to introduce her to us... they seemed very happy together."

"Sara told me about Ibrahim's cousin... Tareq... Maybe..."

The woman's face changed again. She spun toward Samira and gave her a fierce look that seemed to say, "Stop right there." But Samira continued, unperturbed.

"Apparently there was tension between Tareq and your son..."

Mrs. Awad frowned. Her voice was low and menacing. "What are you insinuating?"

"Nothing... I simply thought—"

"Leave Tareq alone. He has nothing to do with this business. It's not enough that the police are harassing me, now you're sticking your nose in it, too"

Her face, ashen a moment earlier, took on a reddish hue. A few beads of sweat appeared at her hairline and slid, like strings of pearls, down her temples. Her hands trembled with anger.

"Listen," Samira began again in an overly restrained voice, "I'm not accusing anyone; I'm just trying to understand. Sara disappeared suddenly, without telling a soul. Ibrahim, too. Tareq is his cousin. Maybe he knows—"

"He knows nothing! I already told you, stay out of this! Tareq wouldn't hurt anyone. How dare you suggest otherwise?"

Choked with rage, the woman could hardly breathe. She cast a last glance at Samira and Daniel, a look full of bitterness, contempt and hate. Then she stood and walked over to the window, turning her back on them. Her voice was nothing more than a grim rumbling, scarcely audible: "Now go away. Please. Just leave me alone."

*

Jerusalem, February 11, 2009

*I had lunch with Ibrahim today. This time, he came to sit at my table.
Samira was leaving just as he arrived. I introduced them and as she
left the cafeteria, Samira gave me a look that was hard to read. Was
she trying to say that he's "an odd sort, but rather pleasant"? Or did
she mean, "Be careful, I don't have a good feeling about this"?*

*Ibrahim sat down and immediately started asking me about
Samira: where she comes from, what she's studying, how long we've
known each other. Perhaps he got the feeling from her smile and the
few words she said to him that there was a hint of judgement, and he
was trying to better understand the person he was dealing with.*

*Then we started talking about movies and directors that we like:
Rohmer for me and Bergman for him. He had just seen* Winter
Light, *a disquieting film about faith that he described with a
tormented enthusiasm, as if he himself had experienced the priest's
questioning. "You understand," he explained, "It's not just God's
silence that the priest, Tomas, finds unbearable. It's the aberration
that God had become within him. An indifferent God, who can do
nothing for humanity, ends up becoming a monster, a spider-god. To
protect Him, so that He doesn't entirely disappear, Tomas must resign
himself to turning his God into a minuscule, personal god who has
no concern other than his own existence as a man and is of no value
to anyone else. Thus Tomas becomes powerless as well: faced with a
man who announces his intention to commit suicide, Tomas can only
confess his own anguish. He is the prisoner of a poor god that he
alone possesses and who banishes him from the world."*

*As he was describing the film, Ibrahim's speech improved. He
still stumbled over certain words, but he was so completely focused on
his story that he forgot himself somewhat and no longer avoided my
eyes. I didn't know how to respond to him. I know nothing about
Bergman or these metaphysical questions. The only Bergman film I've
ever seen is* Fanny and Alexander, *and I only vaguely remember it:*

two martyred children and an enchanting setting. So I smiled. It was a smile without meaning, a smile to fill the silence and to encourage him to continue. But Ibrahim didn't understand. Perhaps he thought that I was laughing at him, that I found his scholarly musings ridiculous.

"But I'm boring you with these stories. I'm sorry, sometimes it gets the best of me and I get carried away." I was about to protest, but with a flick of his hand, he made me see that it was pointless. "You know, I have a tendency to think a bit too much. It's one way to benefit from my flaws: I stutter, yes, I'm shy and awkward, perhaps, but at least I have ideas!"

He rested his elbows on the table and, after tilting his head close to mine, he told me this story: "I used to spend my summer vacations with my aunt in Tira. I didn't get along very well with my cousins. Their war games bored me and I preferred to stay in my corner doing puzzles or building cars with Lego. To retaliate, my cousins nicknamed me 'the philosopher.' I didn't know any more than they did what this word meant, but what it implied – great ideas, serious questions and an immense solitude – fit me rather well. Instead of complaining, I voluntarily accepted this 'insult.' My indifference infuriated my cousins, so they rechristened me 'the failed philosopher.' Ten years later, I was registered in the philosophy program at Hebrew University. After several years of fruitless struggle, I realized that I would never find, in the brouhaha of my mind, the rigour and method necessary for becoming a true thinker. I ended up quitting and, by a strange twist of fate, I actually did become a failed philosopher."

I hadn't expected this confession. Ibrahim smiled and I was surprised to recognize a calm, cheerful pride in his eyes. As if he knew that by revealing his vulnerability, he would arouse not only my sympathy but my admiration as well.

Jerusalem, February 13, 2009
Ibrahim has a cousin, Tareq. They almost never speak to each other. When Ibrahim goes back to see his parents in Nazareth every other

weekend, Tareq barely says hello to him. At the table, he pretends to ignore him but never misses an opportunity to berate "those collaborators who get all chummy with Jews, those fawning Arabs who, because they study at the university, dream that one day they'll be treated as equals." These scarcely veiled attacks no longer bother Ibrahim. He used to try to debate with Tareq even though he never expected to convince him of anything. Now, he retreats into indifference.

Jerusalem, February 15, 2009
"How's your friend?" At first I didn't know what Samira was hinting at. Then she smiled mischievously and I understood. She was talking about Ibrahim. My friend? The word seemed strange. Ibrahim and I often eat lunch together; we share a lot of confidences and I trust him. Does that make him a friend? I feel like the word doesn't suit us well; we need another term, more hesitant and less definitive, one marked by more possibility, perhaps.

❉

From: Daniel
To: Sara
Subject: Retrospective
Monday, February 16, 2009 9:12 p.m.

Dearest daughter,
Do you remember Patrick Brisson, director of Galerie Octo-puce in Old Montreal? The one you called Gargamel when you were little, because he always wore the same black overcoat and rubbed his hands together when he laughed? He's interested in my "imaginary maps of the world" series again and wants to organize a retrospective next fall. I thought about Mama and how happy she would have been. She's the one who gave me the idea about painting maps of made-up countries.

And you, how are your classes?
Your loving father

※

Jerusalem, February 17, 2009

Ibrahim talked about Tareq again. They were raised together as brothers, but Tareq is actually his cousin. Ibrahim's family took him in after his parents died.

At first, the two boys got along fairly well. They were the same age, played the same games, and Ibrahim, who was surrounded by sisters, found in Tareq a companion and accomplice. For the first time, he didn't have to beg his older sister Nouria to play soccer in the yard while waiting for mealtime. And when one of the females in the family – his aunt or a cousin – rebuffed him with the excuse that he was "too young to understand," he no longer felt quite so alone. On Friday nights, when Ibrahim's mother thought they were asleep, the two boys looked at big picture books in the halo of a flashlight or tiptoed down the stairs to spy on the adults drinking coffee in the living room.

Ibrahim's mother treated them as equals. If she felt a difference in her heart, nothing in her words or deeds gave her away. She served the two boys the same dishes, reproached them in the same way when they dawdled in the morning, gave them each a kiss on the forehead when she tucked them in at night. When it came time to celebrate their birthdays, she took care to bake them the same cake, and Tareq had never felt that his gifts were of less value than those Ibrahim received. Sometimes, when she caught them arguing, her desire to remain impartial caused her to side with Tareq, even if he was wrong, simply because she feared that her maternal love would make her appear unjust.

Ibrahim paused and looked at me without smiling. This was his way of making sure he wasn't boring me. We'd been talking for over an hour, sitting by the window in the university cafeteria. Most of the students had returned to class, and I should have resumed my reading at the library long ago. I thought about the essay that I have to turn in tomorrow, but I easily convinced myself that I'd still have time to buckle down and do it, that one more sleepless night wouldn't matter, and so I signalled to Ibrahim to continue.

In elementary school, he explained, he endured his classmates' teasing. His pronounced stuttering earned their mockery and out of necessity, Ibrahim found comfort and safety in silence. To help him ignore the other children, he always kept a book on hand and as soon as someone came to bother him, he buried his nose in it. But this tactic only enflamed his classmates' cruelty: "Watch out, mustn't disturb the intellectual, he's reading!" Ibrahim had to concentrate hard, his eyes vacantly staring at the same sentence, the same word. His will, unshakeable when it came to solving a math problem or learning a long poem by heart, remained powerless against the ridicule washing over him.

Tareq's arrival changed everything. His father had died during the riots at the Al-Aqsa Mosque in October 1990. Tareq was five at the time. Six years later, his mother fell gravely ill and before she died, she entrusted her son to her sister, Ibrahim's mother. At school, the newcomer immediately found his place. Son of a martyr, he aroused both his teachers' sympathy and his friends' admiration. He was forgiven all his escapades, and when he acted a little too arrogant or was rude to a schoolyard monitor, the slate was easily wiped clean. Rather than isolating him, his fierce and independent nature encouraged the boys to include him in their games and the girls to seek his company. In the cafeteria, even when he chose to sit alone, one or another of his pals soon came to join him.

His aura spilled over onto Ibrahim. He was no longer the stutterer, the solitary intellectual, he was Tareq's cousin. His classmates still looked upon him with suspicion, but they didn't dare tease him openly. The insults whispered in the hallways – "filthy teacher's pet" and "stupid loser," among others – had stopped, and the children simply ignored him, which suited Ibrahim just fine.

Of course, Ibrahim's dignity did not come without a certain ambivalence. He benefited from his cousin's popularity (even the girls seemed less hostile toward him), but now he had to share with Tareq his parents' affection – especially that of his mother, with whom Ibrahim was very close. He was no longer unique in that love. But instead of resisting or reclaiming his place, Ibrahim preferred to withdraw into his books. When his father suggested they play some soccer, he didn't refuse, but his heart wasn't in it anymore. If Tareq joined them and wanted to be on his father's team, Ibrahim offered no objection. Was he tired of playing goalie? Perfect, Ibrahim would take over. Did Tareq claim to have scored a goal when the ball had rolled a foot outside the post? Not a problem! Ibrahim let him win every time. It seemed improper, even dishonourable, for him – the first born, the "true son" – to compete with his cousin to win the compassion or esteem of his own parents.

As for Tareq, he did not hide the admiration he felt for Ibrahim. In most matters, he lagged far behind, and he turned to his cousin rather than to his teachers when he didn't understand a math problem. Ibrahim made Tareq review his lessons, reread his compositions and correct his mistakes. Without abusing his authority, he took his teaching role seriously, proving to be by turns enthusiastic, encouraging and impatient.

Ibrahim told me that up until the age of 13, mutual dependence kept them closely connected. And then – here he hesitated, his eyes clouded over and he began to stutter again – Ibrahim was accepted by a well-respected school in Haifa. Its curriculum was based on the sciences and it opened the door to the best universities in Israel. Ibrahim boarded there and only returned to Nazareth every other weekend, and that's when the misunderstandings between the two began.

It was late. The cafeteria was almost deserted and a waiter was making his rounds of the tables and stacking chairs while another followed with a damp mop. Ibrahim seemed fascinated by their monotonous back-and-forth, and I don't know if the sadness in his eyes came from his contemplation of those empty mechanical movements, repeated day after day, or from the memory of Tareq, whom he perhaps could never admit having abandoned.

❅

From: Sara
To: Daniel
Subject: Retrospective
Wednesday, February 18, 2009

Hi, Papa.

I'm so happy about your retrospective. Give me the dates, I'd love to come.

Yesterday, I went out to dinner with Samira. She'd had another fight with her father. He is full of contradictions. He wants her to continue her education and to have a career (preferably as a lawyer) and at the same time, he's hell-bent on marrying her off to a boy from a "good family." Whenever she goes to eat at her parents' house, it's the same story: "So-and-so just graduated from dental school, he comes from an old Jerusalem family, his father owns two hotels. We invited him for tea next week…"

Samira has no intention of getting married, certainly not to any of the candidates her parents are suggesting. Her father must feel that she's slipping away and that it's his last chance to find her a "suitable husband."

I tried to comfort her as best I could. And told myself how lucky I am.

Kisses,

Sara

❅

Daniel had been sitting on The Djerba Palace's terrace for almost 10 minutes. Dragging her feet a bit, the waitress wandered from table to table and didn't appear to be in a hurry to take his order. On the other side of the terrace, Avner sat at a table with friends and spoke with a great deal of animation. His hands drew big circles, whirled around like marionettes, stopped on the shoulders of his companion – an older man who might have been his father – and finally landed on his fiancée's hips. A good audience, she responded to Avner's jokes as she caressed the back of his neck, and his smile, hovering in the shadows, reminded Daniel of the Cheshire Cat in *Alice's Adventures in Wonderland*, which he used to read to Sara on summer evenings.

When he raised his head to call the waitress, Avner finally noticed Daniel and his face darkened. He quickly turned toward his guests, excused himself, absentmindedly dropped his napkin in a bowl of soup and resolutely walked toward Daniel. An austere, worried expression replaced the happy face he'd had a minute earlier. His open hand held before him like a bayonet, he welcomed Daniel and immediately asked, "So, Mr. Benzaken, is there any news?"

"No, not really."

Avner sat and pulled his chair closer to Daniel's. "Did you speak to the detective again?"

"Yes, we talk almost every day. Still no leads."

Avner crossed his legs and put his elbows on the chair's armrests. His face seemed more relaxed.

"But over the past few days, I've met a few of Sara's friends. Some of them told me about you."

At this, Avner frowned and Daniel continued. "It seems Sara cared a lot about you. According to one of her friends, you were even her 'Mr. Right.'"

As he spoke, Daniel studied Avner's face and detected a growing uneasiness.

"She suffered a lot when you broke up. She shut herself up in her room, she stopped going to class and she hardly ate anything."

Daniel observed Avner, whose hard, impenetrable expression gave him the look of a prisoner forcing his face to remain impassive.

"She had a hard time accepting that you had left her – but look," Daniel added, "I'm not blaming you in any way."

Daniel imagined the swirling emotions, the frustration, confusion and anger pressing against the rigid mask that had replaced Avner's face. Unperturbed, Daniel added, "Her friends even told me that she was calling you every day, sometimes late at night. You didn't answer, but she still wouldn't give up. It became sort of an obsession... She wouldn't talk about anything but you..."

Daniel left it at that. No point in going further, the other man had understood.

"What kind of game are you playing, Mr. Benzaken?"

Avner smiled sadly. He hadn't been trusted; he'd been taken for a dirty liar.

"You're right, I haven't told you everything. When Sara and I split up, I didn't believe it was over right away. I kept calling. I wanted to see her again, to talk to her. I wanted to give us a second chance, understand? I don't know what her friend, that... What's her name? Oh, yeah, Samira... I don't know what this Samira told you. Probably that I didn't accept the break-up, that I was harassing Sara, that I was calling her night and day. Am I right?"

"Yes. And then... There's also the anonymous letters."

Avner knit his brows and spread his arms in a gesture of bewildered impotence. "Look, here, Mr. Benzaken, just what do you take me for?"

Daniel was caught off-guard. Surreptitiously, without him noticing, the tables had been turned. He was no longer the accuser but the accused. Now he was on trial and had to defend himself. He had unjustly suspected an innocent man.

"Mr. Benzaken," Avner began again in a generous, almost paternal tone, "You shouldn't be hard on yourself. I understand you very well. You've had no news about Sara and you're worried. I am too, believe me. Lately Sara... I told you, she's been keeping some odd company. This Ibrahim, his family... have you spoken to the police about them? Maybe that's where you should be looking."

Avner stood and prepared to go back to his friends. He extended his hand to Daniel. His grip was strong and confident. But his smile – so genuine, so complete, so unwavering – was it not, in fact, the sign that he was hiding something?

※

Daniel had gone around the corner and was about to get into a cab when he felt a hand on his shoulder. The young woman didn't say a word but signalled that he should follow her. She led him into a narrow alley. In the dimly lit space between the two buildings, Daniel could see the faded colours of sheets drying on clothes lines. He also noticed the black eyes, the indolent gaze finding his face, the mouth whose redness emerged from the darkness like a ripe fruit emerging from murky sea-green water.

"I know about your daughter," said the stranger in a rushed whisper. "I wanted to tell you… I don't know what Avner told you, but when I heard that Sara had disappeared, my first reaction was… You should know that Avner was really in love with Sara. Much more so than he is ready to admit. Now he seems like that – very detached. And in fact since he's been with Rachel, he's doing much better. But right after he and Sara split up, he was inconsolable. Being rejected in one fell swoop, for no apparent reason… he took it very badly."

As she spoke, the young woman constantly looked around as if she were afraid of being seen.

"After they broke up," she began again, "My fiancé, Nathan, went to see him every day. Avner's his best friend and they were in the army together. Frankly, what he told me scares me. Avner talked about getting revenge; he was filled with hate. Especially after he found out that Sara was with that Muslim student… He called him 'the Arab.' One night, I was with them. Avner had been drinking. You had to hear him. He told Nathan everything he wanted to do to the guy. It was horrifying… I don't know, maybe it was just idle threats, but even so… And when I learned that both of them had disappeared—"

119

"Did… did you tell the police about this?"

"Yes, of course. But when I saw you talking to Avner, I thought… Well, you're Sara's father, and you should know."

The young woman nervously glanced at both ends of the alley, took a pen out of her bag and wrote her name – Lola – and her telephone number on a scrap of paper and gave it to Daniel.

"I have to go or they'll get suspicious. Please don't hesitate to call."

❋

Jerusalem, February 19, 2009

Last night, walked with Ibrahim in the Jewish Quarter. We stopped in front of a gallery window. The paintings, all by the same artist, were of ladders linking a dark, hazy ground with an equally dark, cloudy sky. Between the two, a backdrop of ghostly cities, grey and scorched. The canvases all looked alike, the only difference being the ladders, which sometimes leaned to one side, sometimes to the other. I couldn't help but laugh at them, sarcastically elaborating on the highly symbolic tenor of these illustrations of the human tragedy, the impossible alternative between a ruined earthly existence and an even blacker paradise. Ibrahim stepped away to study the rest of the paintings and as he came back to me, he simply said, "I don't know. I don't think it's as bad as all that." At first I thought he was joking too and that he wanted to get me to keep walking, but no, he was completely serious. He looked at me, not in reproach but with a touch of disappointment, the way my mother had when I used a bad word and she'd just frown at me.

I realize that Ibrahim very rarely criticizes anyone. He never says, "That film was absolutely awful" or "This professor is a total bore." He always tries to find value in the effort, no matter how negligible it might be. He finds the tiniest spark, the fragment of sincerity that makes the rest appear worthy. It's not because of his generosity or his belief in the so-called genius of man but because he has so little confidence in himself that he dares not sit in judgement.

Jerusalem, February 20, 2009
For the first time in several weeks, I thought about Avner again. He'd so completely disappeared from my mind that I was no longer even afraid he would call me. But tonight, as I was walking through Nahalat Shiva with Ibrahim, I was suddenly afraid that Avner would see us. This wasn't a totally absurd idea: Avner and I had occasionally eaten at Luigi's, a restaurant in that same neighbourhood. Was he there now with the girl who was my successor, assuming there was one? I pictured him coming out of the restaurant at any moment or appearing at the corner of the street. I imagined his surprise, the look of consternation, anger and contempt on his face, and then I imagined his grin, the generous but inane smile that he displayed for the customers in his restaurant or his mother's girlfriends. I quickened my pace, pulling Ibrahim along with me. I made excuses, saying I was cold and wanted to hurry home, but I don't think he believed me. Why did the idea of running into Avner scare me so much? Is it because I blame myself for letting myself be drawn into a relationship that I scarcely believed in? Do I regret not having ended it sooner, which would have saved him useless heartache? Or is it actually the memory of that wild car ride that still haunts me? His eyes like someone possessed, his silence, his gaping grimace burning with bitter disappointment and hate.

❀

Samira fell asleep in the bus taking them to Khirbet Qeiyafa. Daniel was eager to get to the archaeological site, which both Sara and her friend Tamar had discussed. Who knew? Might he find some indication that Sara had gone back there? Had she taken Ibrahim there? And even if he found nothing, even if the area was deserted, Daniel would still feel a bit closer to her because he would know this place that she loved.

Daniel could not stop looking at the sleeping face beside him. He no longer had to respond to its smile, no longer had to speak. He was free to let his eyes slide over the amber cheeks and the habitually worried forehead that now wore a veneer of calm.

This face, which harboured a thousand memories that came by stealth to lodge there, no longer belonged to Samira. The taboo lifted, it became Sara's sleep that he contemplated, in Montreal, when he used to rise at dawn and wander into her room before preparing his brushes.

He absentmindedly took a pencil from his pocket and put his sketchbook on his knees. Little by little, the features were defined, resembling those that Daniel had so often drawn. Like a haven, they bore the serenity of smiles that had once enveloped him in the apartment on Édouard-Montpetit Boulevard and filled his thoughts as he fell asleep late at night. From his gestures emerged the curve of the chin, the arch of the brows, the peace and torment of the eyes, just as the fevered imagination of the blind man gives birth to the shapes that his fingers caress.

The bus slowed down; Samira awoke. From the corner of her eye, she noticed the drawing and looked over at Daniel. Imperceptibly, her lips reproduced the smile of the face he had drawn. Daniel read her mind: "Is that me in the drawing?"

❋

Jerusalem, February 22, 2009
Ibrahim and I spend most of our time together.
And when we're not together, I think about him.

Jerusalem, February 23, 2009
"We are always waiting for the sign, the revelation that will finally open our eyes and turn us toward God. But for the one who is ready

to listen, the turning has already happened. You don't need to be transformed. You are always facing Him, even when you think you have turned away. Just close your eyes and your voice will find the way all on its own."

When he is tired of talking, Ibrahim writes these little notes on paper napkins from the café where we go to relax after class. Tucked away on a narrow lane in West Jerusalem, the place – called Oo-lye (the Hebrew word for maybe) – attracts the neighbourhood's merchants, retirees and penniless artists. Even though Ibrahim and I go there often, the waitresses barely say hello and always look at us with suspicion. But their poorly disguised hostility doesn't bother us. Why should we change our habits? The place is quiet and they serve the best mint tea, flavoured with orange blossom.

Sometimes we're quiet and simply enjoy an iced coffee and watch the people going by. But usually we talk. He asks a lot of questions about my childhood, my parents and how they met. He listens without smiling, even when I'm trying to be funny. That's because to Ibrahim, who's paralyzed by a stammer that can sometimes hold his voice in suspense for seconds that seem to last forever, conversation is a serious thing. For him, the words, which he has to wrest from his mouth with such incredible effort, have a symbolic, almost mystical significance. When his words are slow in coming, I have the feeling that they are being forged within him for the very first time. And when at last his speech comes, abrupt and chiselled and heavy as a sentence, it's as if it's his opus and belongs to him like his creation, as if it bears the hallmark of his mind.

Jerusalem, February 24, 2009
Sometimes we have to trust our memories, even if they deceive us – and because they deceive us. By altering reality, by leading us down back roads, they tell us about ourselves with a new voice. They make us imagine things that did not exist and, at the same time, they give us a glimpse of things that no longer exist. They rewrite our history and thus become the precursors of our future. It's precisely because

they distort reality, because they model reality on our unknown desires, that our memories have the power to show us our own destiny.

I remember – or think I remember – something my mother said shortly before she died. "Don't stop praying. Even if you no longer feel the need, even if God seems infinitely far away, even if your heart is empty." Mama knew she was going to die and was anticipating my sense of abandonment and betrayal. She sensed that my reaction would be to turn away from God. At least, that's what I once believed. But as I reconsider her last days in the hospital and the conversations that we had, it now seems unlikely that she could have uttered words that so directly referred to her own death. When Papa and I went to visit her, we talked only about my schoolwork, what she was reading (Mama reread the biographies of Schubert and Beethoven when the treatments didn't leave her too weak), and the renovations underway in the apartment. We spoke as if she were going to come home. Mama probably knew that I had understood but didn't want this knowledge to cast a shadow over our last moments together.

This exhortation not to abandon prayer must have come from a time before her illness. Did it come from one of those vacations we took together when we went to celebrate Eid al-Fitr at her sister's house in Paris? She might have explained that prayer had a meaning of its own, that it was our deeds and not our thoughts that mattered most of all. If this conversation has been shuffled around within my memory to become linked with the last hours I spent with Mama, it is perhaps because I cannot accept the idea that her death was completely devoid of meaning. There absolutely had to be a message attached to it, giving it a significance beyond our comprehension and extricating it from the void. Could it be that this shift reveals a rejection that I fail to acknowledge? Without realizing it, I might be feeling guilty that I had so brutally turned my back on prayer and a voice inside me was cunningly mixing up my recollections as a sort of wake-up call. Despite all my efforts and although I believed I'd been purged of my need for God, I am not free, and my memory has restored this imperative in the guise of Mama's parting words.

The Khirbet Qeiyafa site was a 30-minute walk from the spot where they'd gotten off the bus. It was 5 o'clock in the afternoon, but the sun was still blazing.

Before them, to the east, spread the Valley of Elah. Down below, they could see a few olive trees with their twisted branches, dusty shrubs and, in the distance, a village and houses whose cooking fires emitted smoke that slowly merged with the clouds.

The site was deserted. Wooden stakes planted at two-metre intervals marked off the limits of the former village. Hewn stones, carefully aligned, revealed the existence of dwellings whose walls Daniel tried to imagine. Two long tarp-covered tables stood waiting for the next expedition to bring its share of objects to categorize. Under one of the tables, a few forgotten or abandoned tools: a pick-axe, a knife handle, a brush. Daniel made two tours of the enclosure, lifting the tarps and looking under the tables. He stepped away and finally sat on a rock overlooking the valley. Samira came to join him. As he stared out toward the whorls of smoke vanishing and reappearing in the distance, Daniel broke the silence.

"I don't think Sara came back here."

"No, they must have sought refuge somewhere else."

Daniel didn't want to reflect, evaluate or speculate anymore: should he suspect Tareq, whose mother had reacted so strangely to Samira's questions? Or Avner, who Daniel was certain had not been completely honest with him? Daniel had pondered these questions with Samira so many times, he had shared hypotheses with Detective Ben-Ami so often – what could all this effort lead to in the end?

Samira recalled one of her last conversations with Sara. Sara had explained that since her mother's death, she'd been unable to pray. This was Samira's way of sending Daniel an invitation, slightly awkward perhaps, to confide in her and talk about his daughter.

"It came from her mother, this need, this faith," Daniel explained. "I understood it especially at the end of her life, but for

Leila, prayer wasn't just a way of dividing up the day. Those pauses, five times a day, was more than an obligation, it was a way of being in touch with her inner life, they were an extension of the conversation she was having with herself. It was these innermost thoughts, I think, that she communicated to Sara."

"And the fact that she was Muslim and you are Jewish, that didn't—"

"No, that never separated us. Our families, yes. In fact we were never married. Had I been a believer, we might have had conflicts. But for me, you know, God… It's like a far-off murmur approaching, it keeps getting closer but it never manages to reach me. When Sara was small, she often prayed with her mother in the morning. Seeing them together was very touching. I felt like something was happening, something important, but I couldn't understand it. Like a deaf person at a concert who looks at the faces in the audience and recognizes that some phenomenon is holding their attention, even if he can't be part of it."

Samira's eyes traced the sinuous route leading to the village. Here and there, shortcuts intersected it, leading to a steep passage lower in the valley.

"It's funny, all those paths that cross the road. I wonder what they're for," Samira said in a dreamy voice.

"It makes you think of paths of desire," said Daniel.

"Paths of what?"

"Paths of desire – desire paths. You see them in parks sometimes. They're the rough trails made by people who leave the marked footpaths and cut across a grassy area or a field. Some say these paths are the result of bad urban planning, but I wonder if it isn't simply an expression of nonconformity, a desire for freedom that rebels against the engineers' and architects' obsession with geometry."

Daniel dared not turn toward Samira. He imagined that she was smiling, amused by his professorial explanation. Their eyes converged on the same point, at the bottom of the valley, almost meeting, Daniel thought, and this intangible intimacy comforted him.

"When Sara was little, I used to take her to play on Mount Royal on Sundays. On the western side of the mountain, there are a number of these improvised footpaths, some you can hardly see, others freshly made. Sara was really intrigued and decided to make one of her own. So every Sunday morning for an entire summer, she rode her bike down the slope leading to the cemetery, hoping that others would follow this new path."

"Did she succeed?"

"No, of course not. These desire paths are, by definition, capricious in nature. They don't obey the will of an individual but instead, they follow a sort of collective wisdom. Almost as if, even in the heart of the city, our nomadic instinct hasn't been tamed; as if everywhere we go, we strive to blaze new trails."

"I've never heard of these paths of desire. I don't think you'll find many here."

"Maybe because in this country, insecurity makes people more prudent, more compliant with the rules," said Daniel hesitantly.

"Yes... or perhaps this land has already been crisscrossed by so many paths that there's no room to create any new ones."

The day was coming to an end. The olive trees, which had been sparkling in the sun a few minutes earlier, became mere silhouettes, bent, hook-nosed witches gathering the last of the light. The locusts took over for the cicadas and filled the night with swells of mournful sound. Samira and Daniel had to hurry to get back on the road. They were quiet on the way home. But Samira, troubled and sensing her emotions coming to the surface, suddenly felt close to this man who was, after all, no more than a friend's father. She didn't want or expect anything from him. But it seemed unlikely that one day, sometime in the future, once Sara was found, he would disappear from her life. And when she reconsidered what he'd said earlier, it seemed that his words – pained, lucid and serene – had been spoken about her and for her as well.

❊

Jerusalem, February 25, 2009
Early last Sunday morning, we took the bus to Netanyah. We arrived at the beach with the sunrise.

Despite the wind, we rolled up our pants and walked on the wet sand, sometimes avoiding the sharp-edged shells and sometimes the waves drawing bracelets of foam around our calves.

We talked – about our childhoods, Tareq, what we were reading, our projects. But mostly I remember the silence. We walked side by side, the breeze tousling our hair, and it wasn't the words that brought us together, but the trust that comes when you confide in someone and your secrets, freely given, are no longer even worth the trouble of being revealed.

Sometimes his arm brushed against mine. It would have seemed normal, then, if he'd taken my hand. Who knows? When all the details of that day have faded and gone, perhaps the only thing that I will remember is the altered image of a couple and a long embrace.

Jerusalem, February 26, 2009
There's no expression in his eyes. That ice blue, unnatural and impenetrable… Cats also have that completely silent look, calm and austere. Eyes that say nothing can leave themselves open to all sorts of speculations, they can mould themselves to all fears and cruel suspicions. It's a good thing he has his smile. It's weakness that humanizes his face and, by association, gives his expression a solicitude that seems foreign to him.

Jerusalem, February 26, 2009, 11:30 p.m.
Performance of Ibsen's Brand *in Jerusalem tonight. One line in particular struck me: "The victory of victories is to lose everything. Only that which is lost remains eternal." Maybe this truth especially applies to love: it never survives so well as when it is not (fully) experienced.*

Jerusalem, February 27, 2009

Papa and I spoke on the phone the day before yesterday. He asked the usual questions: How's my thesis going? When do I have to go back to Khirbet Qeiyafa? Am I eating well? I would have liked to talk to him about Ibrahim, but I didn't know where to begin. Our first meeting? Our conversations? David Grossman? It's hard to do over the phone. You can't just say, "I met someone. His name is Ibrahim. I'm happy when I'm with him." Right away, you have to say, "We're not dating yet, I don't want to rush things, it's complicated, he's told me a lot about his life, but I still feel like I don't know anything about him." And then of course Papa would expect the details: "How old is he? Where does he live? What is he studying?" Of course I don't blame him. He always worries, it's his nature. And it's worse now that he's alone.

After Mama died, ensuring my safety became his great project, his duty, the intimate pact that kept him bound to her. If I was invited to a party, I never came home alone, he always insisted on coming to get me. He knew my class schedule by heart, and if one evening I was unfortunate enough to be late getting home, he got so nervous he couldn't eat. When she passed away, Mama left behind a fragile world, full of danger and menace. Our fear of being separated slowly brought both of us closer to death. Each little leave-taking — whether I was taking the bus to school or spending a weekend in the country with friends — became for Papa a goodbye that went unrecognized, looming like the shadow of a separation that could become our last.

❊

From: Daniel
To: Sara
Subject: Faces
Saturday, February 28, 2009, 7:14 p.m.

Dearest Sara,
I hope you are well.

Lately I've gone back to painting faces. All pressed together, one against the other, 30 to a canvas. Each one of them is different, and yet they all end up looking alike. It comes from the look in their eyes, I think. I wasn't immediately aware of it, but this expression – a little lost, sorrowful, compassionate – it's the look Mama had when we'd leave her after visiting her in the hospital. It's strange... Ask me to paint Leila's portrait, from memory, and I wouldn't be able to, but I paint dozens of random faces and all of them have her eyes. Sending kisses,

Papa

✳

Jerusalem, March 1, 2009

I wanted to see Ramallah. All those images, the Intifada, the violence, the children – I wanted to know this place.

At the checkpoint, they made both Ibrahim and me get out of the taxi. The officer, a young man of imposing stature, studied my face for a long time. His stare came and went, stopping first on my eyes, then my mouth and forehead before going back to the pages of my passport, which he turned one by one with his thumb.

"You're together?" Without deigning to look at him, he designated Ibrahim with a nod of his head. "Married? Engaged?" He had instantly categorized me as "Jewish woman sleeping with an Arab." Then he asked a seemingly unrelated series of questions. "Where do you live? How long have you been in Israel? What are you going to do in Ramallah? Do you have family in Jerusalem?" He was looking for the hole in my story. He reopened my passport to the first page: Sara Benzaken-Hashim. He frowned. "Hashim, what kind of name it that?" I pretended I didn't understand and said, "It's my mother's name." He raised his head and looked at me severely. Then, like a teacher struggling to be patient with a dim-witted student, he repeated the question: "What kind of name? Christian? Muslim?" I hesitated. I could have said Christian and he would have immediately

130

let us through. But I was curious and wanted to see his reaction. "It's
Muslim."

"Your mother is Muslim?"

"Yes... was. She died."

"And your father?"

"He's still alive."

"Don't be stupid. Your father, what is he? Jewish, Muslim,
Christian?"

"Jewish."

"And what are you?"

I wanted to say Buddhist but I restrained myself. I felt him
seething; pressing the issue would have been pointless. I'd had
enough of my usual answer – "I'm both" or "I'm neither" – it was too
simplistic. He didn't deserve an easy answer. So I looked at him and
with as much poise as possible, I asked, "Why? Is it important?"

He let out an exasperated sigh, turned to look at his colleague
and turned his back on us as he handed me my passport.

In the taxi, Ibrahim watched me from the corner of his eye.
He was smiling.

❋

It was 4 o'clock in the afternoon. Samira had been waiting for
over an hour. Sitting in a café some 30 metres from the Awads'
home, she watched the front door. When Tareq came out, she
would follow him. She had no specific plan. No stratagem, no carefully laid trap. All she wanted was to learn more about him. If circumstances lent themselves, she might approach him and try to
engage him in conversation.

A young man finally left the house. Tall and slim, with a shaved
head: it was definitely the boy that Samira had seen in Mrs. Awad's
family photos. She stood and left the café. The man turned a few
street corners and then when he reached the bus stop, he sat on a
bench. Three other people were waiting – a woman with her child

and an old man with a wizened face. Samira approached the group. Tareq had his nose deep in a book, his eyes half-closed, and seemed to be reciting a prayer. The bus came 15 minutes later. Samira was the last to get on. The only unoccupied seat was the one behind Tareq. As she walked down the aisle, her sleeve brushed the shoulder of the young man, who recoiled like an octopus pierced by a harpoon.

When Tareq stood to get off on El-Bishara Street, Samira followed a little too closely and after taking a few steps, he glanced quickly behind him. Samira hurriedly turned her head to look in the opposite direction, hoping that Tareq hadn't seen her face. Tareq walked toward the Muslim cemetery. Samira gave him time to get farther ahead of her and only continued tailing him after he'd disappeared down a little street just past the Church of Saint Joseph. She crossed the street, picked up her pace, bumped into a passerby – hoping Tareq hadn't entered a house or boutique – but as soon as she turned the corner, she stopped short. With his hands in his pockets and an ironic smile on his lips, Tareq stood waiting for her.

"What are you following me for?"

Frozen in place, Samira looked at him. A shiver ran down her spine like a cascade of icy thorns. Impassive, his expression cold and full of scorn, Tareq repeated his question. "Why are you following me? What do you want from me?"

"I… I'm a friend of Sara's. She and Ibrahim… It's been several weeks since we've heard from them. You're Ibrahim's cousin, right? I thought maybe he'd confided in you—"

Tareq stopped her with a wave of his hand. He spoke calmly, carefully articulating every syllable as if he were speaking to an old woman who was hard of hearing.

"I don't know anything about Ibrahim. We haven't spoken to each other in years. You'd be better off asking people who know him."

His face pale and his forehead already wrinkled, Tareq's hollow cheeks prophesied the old man he would become. His forced smile, cold and affected, bore the weight of the end, of the predestined failure.

"He has nothing but contempt for me," Tareq continued. "Why would he have told me about his plans? For all I know, they eloped and then ran off to celebrate their honeymoon."

Samira was afraid. Afraid of what she believed he was capable of doing. Afraid, too, of his bitterness, his pain, the closed arc of his future and his expression, devoid of desire.

"I know you weren't getting along well…" Samira began again, her voice husky.

But she couldn't go on. If she was going to worm anything out of him, she would have to get him to trust her, lead him to neutral territory. She realized now that she'd made a mistake. She shouldn't have followed him or intimated that she suspected him.

"Weren't you the one who visited my mother a few days ago?"

"Yes, I was," Samira answered, with less assurance than she would have liked.

"I thought so. She told me about you and your little investigation. You checked me out, didn't you? And of course you swallowed every bit of gossip you heard about me: Tareq, he's not all there, he's a fanatic, an extremist, a raging lunatic. He's obsessed with Ibrahim, eaten up with jealousy, and he's full of hate. So naturally he's guilty."

"I'm not accusing you," Samira protested. "You don't understand… All I want is to find out what might have happened—"

Again, Tareq interrupted her. "Oh yeah, right. The truth is that you're just like all the others. You think like them. Someone disappears, so blame it on the Arab. Don't bother looking any further."

Samira turned her head away, unable to endure his stare. What if he was right? Tareq, his rivalry with Ibrahim, his jealousy, his hostility toward Jews – all this clearly makes him guilty, doesn't it? And wasn't she, Samira, as influenced by the same prejudices as everyone else?

At last, Samira raised her head, ashamed. She expected to see Tareq's lips forming the same ironic smile he'd had earlier, but it was gone, only to be replaced by an expression of world-weary satisfaction. His eyes, however, had lost none of their violence. They glittered with rage, power and victorious spite, like the look in Moses' eyes when he contemplated the earth opening up beneath the feet of the traitor Korah.

Samira was too flustered to tell whether this hatred came from a man used to being unjustly accused or from a guilty man who knows he has nothing left to lose.

❈

Jerusalem, March 3, 2009
Avner called me today. I agreed to have a coffee with him. I didn't tell Ibrahim.

He was agreeable, smiling, chatty — he seemed less nervous than he used to be. I felt his breath on my face, an exhalation of cigarette and onion. I remembered the night he first kissed me, when I still thought that something would come fill this void, when I absurdly hoped that my curiosity would evolve into tenderness.

Avner began to tell me every detail of his life since we separated — as if he were answering, a bit against his will, a series of questions I might have asked (How's work? And your father? What do you do in the evening? What movies have you seen lately?). He smiled a lot when he described his vacation — he'd just returned from a week in Prague, he said, leaving an aura of doubt about the person or persons who'd gone there with him.

I listened to him with neither interest nor impatience. I told myself, "So he wants to show me that he's not angry with me, that he doesn't feel any regret or bitterness." He might also have wanted me to keep thinking of him in good terms, to remember him as a man who had briefly been attracted to me, someone who had been generous and had certainly had great hopes for our relationship but who had quickly forgotten me and was now pursuing that relationship, once so full of promise, with someone else.

Then he began to interrogate me. At first, the questions were inoffensive, nothing terribly original. But very quickly, the pace of his delivery increased and his voice became strident. "So you're still single?" I simply nodded. He didn't believe me. "C'mon, you can tell me, you know. I won't be mad." I didn't want to discuss Ibrahim with him. I didn't feel that I was lying to Avner by hiding Ibrahim's existence because, in fact, I don't owe Avner anything. My life is no longer his concern. I'm not obliged to open up to him.

After this first salvo, he seemed to beat a retreat. He took a more conciliatory tone: "You know, Sara, I still think about you… We… what happened? I thought that you and I… I wanted to take you to see Ein Gedi and my grandparents' house. I really thought there was something happening between us – was I wrong? Maybe… maybe things went too fast. If you want…"

It was pitiful. I didn't know how to extricate myself. I was about to answer, "It's not you, it has nothing to do with you. I'm not ready, that's all…" But I thought better of it. His expression had changed again. A pained shadow swept across his face, which had turned cold, agitated and impatient again. "Anyway, you never really wanted… I wasted my time with you. I actually pity you. You'll always be alone, you'll see. Girls like you…"

He hurt me but scared me, too. There was an icy, bitter threat in his voice, a poorly withheld anger. He offered to see me home but I refused. I didn't trust him. I still offered him my hand, although I was somewhat embarrassed, but was relieved when he ignored the gesture. He was content just to smile, his mouth twisted into a sneer.

Jerusalem, March 6, 2009
Supper with Ibrahim's parents in Nazareth.

As he does every Friday before leaving, Ibrahim came to my room to say goodbye. When it came time to kiss me, he hesitated. He looked at me for a long time without smiling and then brusquely asked me to come with him. He must have felt my concern even though I'd done my best to hide it. I said nothing about my meeting with Avner, his

threatening words, his look full of hate. It will pass. I will forget. If
he calls back, if he wants to see me again to apologize, I will ignore
him. Eventually he'll leave me alone. But Ibrahim is no fool. He
understood that something was wrong.

    On the bus taking us to Nazareth, we hardly spoke. I stared out
at the white villages perched on top of sandy hills, the herds of goats
whose bleating seemed a response to the plaintive rumbling of the bus
struggling uphill, the dusty olive trees whose gnarled branches seemed
to suffer from an invisible affliction. Such a landscape should have
carried me far from my thoughts, but Avner's voice, both honeyed and
hostile, still troubled me. "You'll be alone all your life... Girls like
you..." It wasn't this sentence pronounced against me that was so
frightening. It was his mouth warped by rage, his hands crushing
then tearing to pieces the pack of cigarettes lying on the table and
especially his humiliated expression, vibrating with hate.

    Once we were at Ibrahim's, I relaxed a bit. I was touched by the
welcome his parents gave me. We talked about Lebanon, Beirut's
beaches, the dishes that were part of our childhoods – sambousik
jebne, malfouf, fatoush, mouhalabieh. *I was curious about their*
family's history, and Ibrahim's father had started to describe his par-
ents' house in Deir el-Asad, a village in the Galilee, when Ibrahim's
cousin Tareq appeared in the doorway. How long had he been there?
Had he been listening in on our conversation? In any case, I hadn't
heard him come in. He stared at me, and I was about to get up to
shake his hand when he abruptly turned around and stomped toward
the kitchen. Ibrahim's mother quickly followed him, as if she expected
something to break.

    We could hear them arguing all the way in the dining room. The
mother's voice – liquid, unctuous, murmuring – seemed to be trying
to suppress the torrent of anger that Tareq was unleashing on her.
"Who is this girl? What's she doing here? Another one of those smart-
ass intellectuals? How dare he bring that here? Has he no shame?
And you sit there saying nothing?" His voice, sometimes harsh,
sometimes serious, like the mournful modulations of an electric saw,

reminded me of the voice of Rabbi Benchetrit when he was trying to convince us that Israel is our ancestral land and that we have no right to give up even one square centimetre of our territory to the Arabs.

After a bit, Ibrahim's mother returned, alone, to the dining room. She smiled, but her eyes reflected shame and fear. She began to clear the table. When Ibrahim saw that her hands were trembling, he immediately stood, made her leave the dishes where they were and led her into the living room, whispering, "Don't be upset, it's not your fault..." Then Ibrahim came to find me; I thanked his father, who smiled at me forlornly, and we left.

We didn't talk on the bus and we didn't sleep. We watched the villages' shadows and dying lights file past in the humid night. Ibrahim knew all my questions. And his answers, I easily imagined. We had only the fleeting comfort of being together to protect us.

FOR THREE DAYS AND THREE NIGHTS, Abraham walks. The voices inside him are silent.

It is early morning when he finally arrives, throat parched and lips cracked. A diaphanous glow envelops the desert like the evanescent sigh of the voice he so avidly desired.

With heavy legs, Abraham goes to the well. Leaning against its edge, he raises the pail and plunges his head into it. The cool water brings him back to the present.

Behind the tent, he unties the donkey and lets him drink. He collects a few branches and lays them across the animal's back.

His movements are slow and measured, like those of a man completing a task he has long considered.

Then Abraham sits on the sand and, holding a whetstone between his knees, sharpens his knife.

Breaking through the morning clouds, the first rays of the sun fall and die upon his face.

Abraham approaches the tent where Sarah lies sleeping. Isaac, his son, his only remaining son, the son he loves and whose love anchors him to the world, lies stretched out not far from her. He kneels down and lifts his son in his arms.

Outside, Isaac opens his eyes, but Abraham does not look at him.

"Where are we going?" Isaac asks his father.

"We are going where God will show himself. See: I've prepared everything for the sacrifice."

"But Father, I see only the knife and the firewood – where is the lamb?" Isaac asks.

Eyes turned toward the horizon, Abraham answers in a hushed voice, as if talking only to himself, "God will provide what is needed for the sacrifice."

With one hand, Abraham takes the donkey's bridle. He leads his son with the other.

For three days and three nights, they walk, together.

Abraham does not look at Isaac nor does he speak to him. His eyes staring off into the distance, his jaws clenched, he listens.

He listens to their footsteps whispering in the sand, to the wrathful wind buffeting his tunic about, to Isaac's laboured breathing.

On morning of the fourth day, they reach the summit of Mount Moriah.

Isaac helps his father light the fire. He carefully watches each movement his father makes. He studies the face whose eyes, surrounded by wrinkles, seem like mere slits. Abraham has no need to speak: Isaac has understood.

He does not ask why he must die. He will fulfill the will of Abraham.

5

Daniel woke up with a start. As it did every morning, the gaping anguish greeted him even before his eyes had opened. But this time, the dream had left its traces. A weight, on his chest. A body. A life that murmured and breathed. At first, he wasn't sure. Was it a small animal? A cat, perhaps? But guided by the odour, he soon recognized the presence. Sweet, earthy and fresh, a hint of vanilla and cinnamon. The memory reborn: baby Sara. Tormented by colic, she used to wake up at 2 o'clock in the morning. Reeling with fatigue, he would take her from her bassinet, lie down on his back on the floor and place her on his stomach. She would finally fall back to sleep and, calmed by her respiration, so did he.

But in his dream, Sara, the little being, the little presence on his chest, does not sleep. He holds her with all his strength and she struggles. He locks his arms around her, deaf to her cries. She doesn't understand. He has no choice. They want to kidnap her, take her far away from him. He must resist. He knows that he is suffocating her, strangling her, but what else can he do?

As Daniel awoke, the crying continued with its piercing echo, and the body – frail, tiny, immense – still weighed on him, matching his gasping breaths like a cork tossed about by the waves. In this backlit awareness, so close to sinking back into the night, a question rose to the surface: this weight, this life that he had held so tightly just a moment ago, if it still exists, if it has not entirely disappeared, is it not precisely because it is nothing, because it is cut from the indestructible fabric that dreams are made of?

❄

Jerusalem, March 8, 2009
"She says: 'Why do we love then walk on empty roads?' I say: 'To
conquer the plenitude of death with less death and escape the abyss.'"
Mahmoud Darwish

Jerusalem, March 9, 2009
Ibrahim's face. The first time I saw it, in the university cafeteria,
I remembered having seen him before, sitting in the first row in
Professor Barnathan's class. But there was something else. I kept
having the feeling that I'd already met him somewhere. I thought
about it for a long time. Does he look like the son of the rabbi at the
reform synagogue that Papa took me to on holidays? No, maybe they
have the same perplexed look, but that's not it. Maybe it's his smile?
Despite its brightness, it communicates a not-quite-forgotten sadness
that reminds me of a child's smile. But I can't put my finger on it.
All I can say is that it's a smile I desired. But maybe it's his eyebrows,
which are very arched and set in a mournful "alas!" I have carefully
explored the furthest corners of my mind to no avail. Is it perhaps
just this memory, separate from any reality, that makes me love him?
There's this hollowness that I'm trying to fill; I convinced myself that
at first this emptiness was a light, while in truth it was nothing but a
screen that I used to shelter my first desires, the fabricated answers to
my solitude.

There are faces that we recognize and love precisely because
we recognize them (they belong to those closest to us, those who
accustomed us to tenderness and trust). There are faces that we don't
recognize and that remain foreign (most of humanity). And then
there are those that we recognize but have never met. The face is
unfamiliar, impossible to find the least trace of it in our memory,
and yet we feel as if it is part of our life. It is infinitely "other," yet at
the same time, it seems as if we share the same beginnings. Maybe
it's this exclamation, this incongruous juxtaposition, this "it is him!"
superimposed on a "but I don't know him" that makes us believe love
is a destiny. Some would say that it's essentially an error in judgement,

a confusion of our faculties, similar to the kind that makes us call a
sound "red" or that leads a man who's suffered a concussion to call his
wife a hat. Maybe that's the way it is with Ibrahim. I recognized him
and still believe that his face is familiar, but it's just my brain playing
tricks on me.

Jerusalem, March 11, 2009
Ibrahim. I carry your name inside me like an ancient memory.
Perhaps your love for me is nothing more than your own need to
be loved – by me or by someone else. But this love – because it
comes from this sensitive place inside you, because it speaks of
your vulnerable kindness and your fledgling desire to be held,
embraced, enveloped by a stranger's arms – seems immense.
There's a tenderness that will forever go unnamed, that I will
never have adequately understood and that will always take me
back to a first glance.

✳

From: Daniel
To: Sara
Subject: Lecture at Columbia
Wednesday, March 11, 2009, 11:41 a.m.

Dear Sara,
I gave my lecture at Columbia yesterday. Everything went well. The
auditorium was full and I even signed a few books.
That evening, John Bomgrich invited me to have dinner with a few
colleagues at Terrace in the Sky, a restaurant in Morningside
Heights, near the university. It's a pretty strange place: you go into
a building that looks like any other, you go up in a rickety old elevator to the 16th floor and enter a sumptuous dining room surrounded by an immense bay window. Everywhere you look, you see
the city. Very impressive.

I sat across the table from one of Bomgrich's students. He told me about his thesis ("The Notion of Beauty in Pre-Columbian Art"), his trips to Mexico and Peru. He was very eloquent and very touching, too. Listening to him, I thought of you and said to myself, perhaps... You see, I may not be as annoying as Samira's father, but it's still the sort of thing I can't help thinking about!

I send you a big hug.

Papa

❊

Almost every evening, Samira came to meet Daniel in the hotel bar. They had their habits: sitting on a big leather sofa in an alcove draped with heavy curtains, they would share a club sandwich, order two martinis followed by half a carafe of red wine that they made last late into the night. They reported on their day, exchanged their hypotheses, tirelessly repeated the same futile speculations. Sometimes digressions slid them into the realm of memories. From there, they moved on to confidences and little by little, the other's life was built before their eyes into a precarious structure riddled with holes and questions, as imaginary and as poignant as their own past. Strangely, this ambiguity comforted them and gradually convinced them that they had more to lose by protecting their secrets than by letting the other in.

That night, Samira told Daniel about the dream she'd had the previous night.

She is walking, completely veiled, through the streets of Nazareth. A single slit allows her to see without being seen. Samira is not used to this voluminous garment that slows her pace and hinders her movements. She is surprised to discover that men's eyes do not regard her with indifference but rest on her, trying to guess at her shapes and imagine her features and the expression on her face. They observe her, they watch her, they spy on her. Veiled, she is more naked than ever.

In her dream, she gets on a bus and sits next to a man. He turns his head toward her. She recognizes Tareq. Her first instinct is to flee, but a mysterious force holds her back. "Who are you?" The young man is serious, his tone hostile. Samira answers, "I'm Sara. Ibrahim's friend. Your cousin, Ibrahim." What had come over her? Why this lie? Tareq's face seems to crumble before her eyes. He turns pale, his hands tremble, he can hardly breathe. "That's it, it's him! I'm sure of it, he's guilty!" Samira thinks. But Tareq soon pulls himself together. A smile slithers across his face like a snake. "Prove it." Frightened, Samira looks at him. If he could see the look of terror on her face, he would surely burst into a fit of Machiavellian laughter. Tareq insists: "Go on, prove it. Take off your veil." Samira would like to get up, get off at the next stop and run, but she is paralyzed. She looks into Tareq's mocking face where his eyes glitter with cruelty and victorious joy. When she finally stands, her back drenched with sweat, Samira still feels the young man looking at her, his eyes gliding over her skin like slimy water, like a damp, dark veil.

❋

From: Sara
To: Daniel
Subject: Columbia lecture
Thursday, March 12, 2009, 8:15 a.m.

Thanks for your last email, Papa. I'm glad everything went so well at Columbia but please, don't start playing matchmaker!!
I am a bit overwhelmed with work at the moment. We'll speak on Sunday?
Big kiss,
Sara

❋

Jerusalem, March 13, 2009, 9:30 p.m.
I regret losing my patience. It was 6 p.m. We were walking in the
Arab Quarter and I was going to invite Ibrahim to come have supper
at my place but I didn't have the chance. The muezzins were calling
the people to prayer and Ibrahim suggested that I go to the mosque
with him. I refused.

I brusquely said no, without thinking. I said no without thinking
about how Ibrahim would react. I said no because I don't know how
to pray anymore and because I don't like to be among people who
believe.

Jerusalem, March 13, 2009, 11 p.m.
I was wrong. All this has nothing to do with Ibrahim. He has never
doubted. At least not like I have. Not the kind of doubt that makes
you reject everything, that gives you the power to imagine a world of
solitude and strength, a world without God. I told him about my
mother, her illness and her death.

This death, which was first my undoing and which then became
God's. Initially, I told myself that of course, it was my fault. I hadn't
prayed hard enough. I would have had to believe beyond all doubt,
beyond the obvious, that she would get better. But I didn't give myself
over to Him entirely, so He didn't give my mother His full presence
either. It would have been necessary to… I don't even know anymore
what thoughts I'd had in my head back then. I would come home
from school in the evening and like a robot, I'd do my homework
and then make something to eat. After going over my homework one
last time, I'd fall asleep, exhausted, around midnight, and then wake
up around four or five in the morning with a vast abyss gaping inside
me.

I'd prepare for the morning prayers, kneel down as if Mama were
beside me, and my timorous murmur – so worried and uncertain –
would remind me of her voice. I'd recite the same words and repeat
the same movements, as if they'd inserted themselves into the space
carved out by her absence.

Sometimes I'd also read the Kaddish, the Jewish prayer for the dead. Partly to be provocative, since it is a prayer reserved for men, but also because I was seeking consolation. Because I was seeking God, who would say to me, "Your mother… she is watching over you. You are not alone. The dead are with the living. And even though the living do not hear them, their acts and their attentions slip in and help the dead bear the weight of the void."

But what's the use of praising God, exalting His power or glorifying His name when he had turned away from me, when he had failed to protect the thing I held most dear, the one on whom my life and my future depended? What did I have left to hope for from a being who could do nothing for me but who demanded that I give him all my love, all my adoration and my complete submission? For months on end, I had taken refuge in those words and had allowed Him to see inside me, I had recited all the psalms I knew and all the verses of the Koran that Mama had taught me. I had even invented my own prayers in French. Very simple prayers that always began and ended the same way: "Dear God, I beg you, cure my mother…" And should I have kept praying as if nothing had changed, as if my prayers had been answered? Was that what it meant to be faithful to my mother?

After she died, I continued blindly repeating these praises, hoping to find a new meaning that would speak to me of another life, an unexpected hope. But all these words were worse than silence. This string of empty promises did nothing more than parody the fervour that had driven me during Mama's illness. And that immense being that had so faithfully enveloped me in tenderness and compassion? It was nothing but the fiction seen by others, by those who don't believe and never did: a peremptory incantation with no more hold over the world than the "abracadabras" of a fairy tale.

I prayed for Mama to get well. She died and God died along with her.

God, the God that had been with me since I was little and in whom I had placed my trust, would not have let my mother die. God?

That was my mother when she was alive, her smile full of confidence, her eyes that had put an end to fear. God was the order of the world, a world where mothers tucked their children into bed each night and took them to school each morning, a world where love protected and prayer kept death at bay.

※

In the evening, Daniel walked around the Old City until it was time for his meeting with Samira. He hadn't slept in two days; he had hardly eaten. Anxiety was tightening its noose.

Dazed, haggard, and numbed by the heat and the clamour of the street, he walked along with hesitant steps. Here, he tripped on the uneven cobblestones in an alleyway; there, on the verge of collapse, he stumbled in front of a merchant's shop. At his side: Leila. She was his guide, no need for him to know where to go. Leila was with him, and that was enough.

At first, her presence was only a voice. Stripped of words, it was no more than an intuition, an omen, a shadow that would soon resurface but never see the light of day. This Leila, who enveloped him and smiled at him though she had no face, was also the empty space growing inside him, the part of his being exiled so long ago, still vibrant and yet unrecognizable. It was, ultimately, his own future, that which would remain when all was said and done: a gossamer awareness, unburdened by past or desire, an as-yet-unborn life with no understanding of time.

Night was falling. The *muezzins'* chant rose into the air, a victorious lamentation that crashed against the voice of silence. Again Daniel lost himself in another world, transported by his memories.

Sara is six years old.

"How come you never pray, Papa?"

"I don't know how to pray."

"Come, I'll teach you. You'll see, it's easy."

He watches Sara. She touches water to her face, ears, hands, arms and feet. Hesitant, he imitates her gestures. Standing beside her, he whispers, as she does, *"Bismillah ir-Rahman ir-Rahim..."* Then Sara kneels. Daniel does not.

He listens to her, moved by the haunting modulations she is making with her breathless voice. Sara stops, stands and turns toward him with a look that seems to say, "So, what are you waiting for?" Daniel spreads his arms, miming helplessness. "I can't." Then offers an explanation: "When you're Jewish, you know... we aren't allowed to prostrate ourselves..." Disconcerted, Sara looks at him for a moment and then resumes her prayer.

Later, Sara finds him in the living room, sits near him and lays her hand on his arm. "It's not a problem, you know. You don't need to pray. You have your painting."

Daniel regained his composure. Why had he let himself get carried away again? The slightest thing was enough to unshackle the phantoms of the past. One image leads to the next; we think we're running away but in fact we're sinking deeper, getting entangled, trapped in our memory's web. For Daniel, every recollection was a betrayal, a little bit of life he was taking from Sara. Seeking her in the past meant accepting that he would not find her again.

❊

Jerusalem, March 14, 2009
Right now, I'm reading the diary of Etty Hillesum, a Dutch Jew who died in Auschwitz when she was 29 years old. Toward the end, she speaks directly to God: "I shall try to help You, God, to stop my strength ebbing away, though I cannot vouch for it in advance. But one thing is becoming increasingly clear to me: that You cannot help us, that we must help You to help ourselves. And that is all we can manage these days and also all that really matters: that we safeguard that little piece of You, God, in ourselves."

Jerusalem, March 15, 2009

I told Ibrahim about Mama. He looked at me without emotion. After a long silence, he simply said, "You know, you don't have to believe in God to pray."

And then, as he so often does, he changed the subject – so suddenly that I wondered if he'd really heard what I'd just said. He started talking about the character of Abraham in the Torah and the Koran. He didn't understand the story of the "sacrifice." God wanting to test Abraham by demanding that he kill his son? It's absurd. If that really was all it was about, Abraham was nothing but a fool, not a man of God. There must be more to it.

Ibrahim took a big folder out of his knapsack. It was filled with papers delicately handwritten in green ink. He came to sit on the floor next to me, leaned against the sofa and placed the papers on his knees.

"Here, I'm going to read you a story: 'For a long time, Abraham lived, and every day the voice of God expanded the scope of his awareness a little more. After years of plenitude, however, questions forced their way in. The presence of His words was no longer enough for him. He asked for a sign...'"

It was the story of Abraham and his son Isaac. In Ibrahim's story, Abraham is tortured by doubt. He confronts God, begs Him for an answer, but remains a prisoner of his solitude. Then, a distraught Abraham threatens to kill the dearest thing in the world to him – his own son – to force God into giving him an indisputable sign of His existence. It is Abraham who tests God, and not the other way around.

When I woke up this morning, I lingered and watched Ibrahim as he lay stretched out on the floor asleep. But I couldn't recapture the comfort I'd felt last evening, his voice warm and unchanging, as if it had emerged from the spreading night. And of his story, so full of life and so complete a few hours ago, there remained, in my fading memory, nothing but a series of hopeless enigmas, a rhapsody of resonant but aimless, disconnected words.

Jerusalem, March 17, 2013

"God only appears to us when we have nothing left. He is this last hope, this tiny light when the world is on the verge of giving way beneath our feet."

Ibrahim was reading me the story of Job, his struggle against God, his fight to keep God from disappearing.

"You're too unwilling to compromise. You wanted God to follow your every step, to be with you and set you on the right path like some kind of guardian angel. If our life was so full of certainties, why would we need God? Praying has meaning, even if we're not sure – and because we're not sure – that God hears us. You'd like prayer to be effective; you'd like it to change the world. But you're the one who has to be changed by prayer. The one you invoke and that you call God, you'd like Him to move all the pawns on the chessboard, to listen to you and allow you to guide Him. But it may not be within His power to awaken even the slightest breeze or extinguish the tiniest spark. All you can hope for is that through your own determination, He'll lead you far from the noise to a place where reason is no longer of any use to you. He'll be the journey home that will finally turn you away from the chessboard, because the battle that counts lies elsewhere. No, He didn't save your mother. But instead of being angry at Him, shouldn't you sympathize with Him instead? Because in the end, perhaps He's the one who needs to be saved.

Jerusalem, March 18, 2013

I listened to Ibrahim.

If God is to come back to me, I have to rid myself of everything I know about Him.

He did not create the world. He is not all-powerful. He does not cure those who are sick. He does not observe my every move. He does not judge people. He does not punish them. He does not answer prayers. He does not console us in the face of death.

*I shouldn't even say "God" anymore. Every time I invoke God,
I should open up a silent space in the words. I should write "   "
to signify "God."*

*He is what I have left when I've lost everything: the dying,
almost-extinguished strength to still want Him to answer me. It is
then, perhaps, that He'll welcome our attention: when we have
abandoned hope, when love has betrayed us, when everything
conspires to chase Him from our thoughts. Arisen from the ruins,
He is my voice that still calls out and, in my voice, He is the
continuity of the living.*

Jerusalem, March 19, 2009
God, without the trust.

Jerusalem, March 20, 2009
*God reveals Himself in the tiny opening left by doubt – in the
suspicion that He could, after all, rise to the surface of my awareness,
despite the overwhelming evidence of his absence.*

*Exiled from the world, I am, in the world, the memory of His
presence.*

❄

From: Daniel
To: Sara
Subject: Jerusalem
Friday, March 20, 2009, 10:51 p.m.

Dear Sara,
I bought my ticket this morning. I arrive May 25. I can't wait!
Big kisses,
Papa

❄

On Sunday, Daniel and Samira ate at the Three Arches Hotel. Before accompanying Samira back home, Daniel suggested that they go up into the tower.

Leaning their elbows on the parapet, they let the hum of the city lull them and recognized, in the heavy, bitter emanations rising into the air, the life of the streets and gardens below. Daniel's gaze fell on the young woman's face, on the curve of her bare back, which arched like a figurehead's, and on her eyes, which were fixed on the horizon. Bathed in sunlight, her eyes seemed to borrow their colour from the amber of the city and the earthy luster of the stone. Her irises, burning bronze embers, seemed to twinkle, falling on Daniel as if on the surface of the sand in an hourglass.

Samira turned her head toward Daniel and he immediately stopped looking at her. His eyes fell to the foot of the tower, 25 metres below. Samira was afraid. She thought she recognized in his expression not the shame of having observed her with too much urgency, but the inertia of a man who is about to throw himself into the void.

❋

Jerusalem, March 22, 2009
Avner just called. I'm scared.

"I saw you with the Arab." How did he know? It's obvious he's been following me.

For how long? Where did he see us? At the dorm on Mount Scopus?

There was so much hate in his voice... It's as if I didn't recognize him, as if I'd never known him. I could tell that he'd been drinking. He repeated his accusation: "I saw you... I know everything..."

I can still hear that hushed voice sounding like a man possessed. I could almost see his face, his petulant, sarcastic smile, his sticky lips, and in his eyes that abyss, that silence, that frozen life – like the blankly staring orbs of a Roman statue's eyes.

Bit by bit, I figured out why Tareq and Ibrahim had grown apart. With Ibrahim gone, Tareq no longer had someone to defend against their schoolmates' malevolence, someone to help him at school and give him the confidence he lost after Ibrahim's departure. As for Ibrahim, he had discovered a whole new world. When he returned home from Haifa, he would enthusiastically describe his school, his professors, his classmates – the majority of whom were Jewish. He was discovering areas of interest that had until then been completely unknown to him: the history of mathematics, the French Revolution, the digestive system of mammals. Authors whose names he hadn't known – Shakespeare, Dickens, Molière – were gradually becoming less foreign.

But most importantly, he was learning Hebrew. As he read the Bible for the first time, he grappled with new incarnations of figures from the Koran: Abraham, Ishmael, Jacob and Moses. The story of Joseph and his brothers took a strange yet familiar turn: it was like suddenly hearing music for violin played on the piano. The two narratives, one from the Torah and the other from the Koran, seemed to develop, in different keys, two variations of a single theme that neither one fully encompassed.

In the beginning, he tried to share these impressions with Tareq, but Tareq turned out to be so hostile that Ibrahim chose not to insist. He spent more and more time with his friends in Haifa and only went home to Nazareth every other weekend. He still confided in his mother, but he only exchanged polite questions and benign comments with Tareq.

At college in Haifa, Ibrahim became friends with a Jewish student. His name was Elie and he, like Ibrahim, was a scholarship student. The other students made fun of him, his old-fashioned wide-wale cords, his worn-out shoes and his jacket with the threadbare sleeves, but Ibrahim found in him a natural ally. Elie, at least, didn't think Ibrahim's accent was weird (or in any case, he made no comment), nor did he laugh when Ibrahim mixed up his Bs and his Ps. They sat together in the library to review their *assignments, discussed their reading and traded CDs of their favourite groups.*

One weekend, Ibrahim made the mistake of mentioning Elie's name at dinner, and for Tareq, that was the last straw. In the beginning, his pride won out and he kept quiet. But Tareq's feelings gradually came to light. He started with poorly veiled allusions to the Jews' duplicity, referring to current political events to prove that you can never trust them. Then he quoted the Koran to remind Ibrahim that a Muslim was forbidden to befriend both Jew and Christian. Though not eager to embark on a theological debate with his cousin, Ibrahim cited another verse from the Koran that calls on believers to love their peers no matter what their origins, but from that moment on, he felt an insurmountable distance separating him from Tareq.

Ibrahim hadn't immediately understood, but Tareq had experienced his cousin's departure as a betrayal. The fact that he was learning Hebrew and developing friendships with Jews and that one of them was even becoming his best friend only enflamed Tareq's anger and jealously. Ibrahim had asked his mother to try to reason with Tareq, but Tareq – believing that she had been sent by his cousin – had only rejected her that much more harshly.

Ibrahim recounted these events with a sort of objective indifference, as if they involved someone else, but I saw that his intense expression reflected his struggle to find the right words. I saw that the wound was still raw and that he felt equally abandoned by Tareq. Reconciliation, he explained, was now made even more impossible by the fact that Tareq was the prisoner of a religious ideology that made any debate a wasted effort. In fact, soon after Ibrahim left, Tareq began attending a night school where they taught the Koran and Islam's main tenets. The radical ideas that Tareq brought home with him strongly suggested that they were doing more in class than reciting verses from the sacred book. Tareq, whose father had died in the riots at the Al-Aqsa Mosque, was easily led in such an environment, where he found a haven and an outlet for his hatred.

As I listened to Ibrahim, I remembered the look exchanged with Tareq when he came and stood in the doorway in Nazareth – an apparition I immediately returned to the world of dreams. Ibrahim's account brought this vision back to life, revealed its meaning to me in the same way that you might discover in its blinding clarity, once the fog had lifted, a landscape whose forms you had only guessed at earlier. Again I saw Tareq's smile marked with spite and unrest and, more importantly, his eyes that seemed to contradict each other, one being kind and caressing and the other tormented by hate. That look of contained rage, of tenderness scorned, silenced and dead yet, in spite of it all, reborn – it seemed to contain their entire story.

❋

The murky blue-grey light of morning broke through the half-open curtains. Daniel closed his eyes again and sleep embraced him once more.

In his hand, a weight, another hand. Leila. They have plans to meet some friends and are walking over Mount Royal to get to the Plateau. Here and there, mounds of snow pocked with twigs and dead leaves dot the muddy paths like the last remnants of a molting skin that spring has yet to slough off. Leila is pregnant, and when the road gets steeper, the pressure of her hand in his grows more insistent. Without this impatient and determined guide, Daniel would be lost. How many times had he taken a wrong turn as he walked around Montreal, despite it being such a generous and accommodating city?

But isn't this hand, which trembles in his like a little animal, too small to be Leila's? In his half-sleep, it is Sara's voice, timid and monotone, that emerges. She is reciting poetry, worried that she doesn't know it well enough, and Daniel does his best to reassure her. The closer they get to her school, the more breathless Sara's recitation becomes. She is sure that she will be questioned on it. She must repeat the last verse without the least little mistake, three times in a row. The small hand in Daniel's grows moist, and when it slips out of his, he tries to hold onto it. But it has already returned to the fragility of dreams. It's no longer Sara's hand, it's…

Daniel opens his eyes. Sleeping at his side, Samira, their hands… Slowly, he remembers. Last night. He'd had too much to drink. Samira had helped him get back to his room where he stretched out on the bed without undressing. She probably hadn't wanted to leave him alone… what had happened afterwards? Was he the one, having lost his bearings and looking for support… or had she, sensing that he was fragile and confused, wanted to comfort him… In a few moments, he would withdraw his hand. Gently, slowly, so as not to wake her. But not right away. A few more seconds of this silence, this presence, his loneliness deferred…

❋

Jerusalem, March 30, 2009, 8:15 p.m.
Avner, again. This time he doesn't say anything. The phone rings.
I answer. He waits. The third time, I say, "Avner, I know it's you.
What do you want? I've said everything I have to say to you… All
this is pointless…" But he doesn't speak. I hear him breathing, that's
all. The seventh time, I get impatient. "Stop it, Avner! I've had
enough! Leave me alone!" My voice trembles. I'm scared. I turn off
my phone, but I know that by tomorrow morning, I'll have 30 calls
from an unknown number.

Jerusalem, March 30, 2009, 10:30 p.m.
A hand on my shoulder. I jumped. It was Samira. I told her what's been
going on. Avner, his venom, the anonymous phone calls… She tried
to reassure me: "He'll get over it. He'll find someone else. He'll forget
you soon enough. And besides, who knows? Maybe it's not even him."
Samira is right. Maybe it isn't Avner. But who, then? It's been
going on for a week, every night starting at 8 o'clock. Ten, maybe 15
times. Until I turn off my phone. And the next day, it begins again. As

if he gets a thrill just from hearing me say, "Hello? Who's calling?"
Just to feel the growing anxiety in my voice, my confusion, my anger.

Samira thinks I should be proactive. Go find Avner, talk to him,
explain to him. But what for? It's not as if I haven't already tried. I
agreed to go have coffee with him, I talked with him as much as I
could. But when he called me, half-drunk, and said, "I saw you with
the Arab…" That threatening tone, that aggression… no, there's noth-
ing I can do.

✻

From: Daniel
To: Sara
Subject: Storm
Tuesday, March 31, 2009, 8:21 a.m.

Dear Sara,
Another storm yesterday. Winter just won't end.
You seemed preoccupied the last time we spoke on the phone.
Is it your schoolwork?
If there's anything I can do, please don't hesitate to ask.
Kisses,
Papa

✻

Jerusalem, April 2, 2009
Ibrahim seemed nervous tonight. We sat in the kitchen and shared
the falafel that he'd bought on the way over here. I wasn't really
hungry and neither was he.

I was worried about how my voice sounded. I felt like it was
giving me away. I hadn't told Ibrahim anything yet. Those damn
telephone calls, Avner's threats — it all might stop and I don't want
to cause him needless worry.

Ibrahim tried to avoid looking me in the eye. He was even quieter than usual. After I questioned him, I finally understood. There were two of them… At first, he thought it was just a coincidence. When he came out of the movie theatre, they were there, posted at the entrance to the café. Two days later, he saw them in a sky-blue Corolla parked in the university lot. The day before yesterday, there they were again – a tall young man, with hunched shoulders and black hair cut close to the scalp, and a potbellied guy with tanned skin and fleshy lips – pretending to search for something in the bookstore where Ibrahim spends his afternoons. And just now, he was certain, the same men had been across from the bus stop, watching him.

Avner. Is he capable of doing such a thing? Having Ibrahim followed? And what's it all for? To scare us? To satisfy his jealousy?

Jerusalem, April 3, 2009
I ended up telling Ibrahim.

Avner. The phone calls that come until late at night.

For a long time, Ibrahim remained silent. Then, in a voice that wasn't his own, a subdued, flat voice that lacked all its usual modulations: "How do you know it's him?"

Jerusalem, April 5, 2009
Ibrahim used my new cell phone to call his mother. I'd gotten rid of the old one. Now no one calls me. Papa and Ibrahim are the only ones who know my number.

Ibrahim was in the kitchen. From my room, I heard bits of his conversation. He was imploring, begging: "You're the only one he listens to… You have to talk to him… He has to stop, otherwise…"

He joined me after he'd hung up. His hand on mine, like a soothing shadow, a pale and sombre silhouette miming my fingers' nervous curve.

Ibrahim felt uncertain. Tareq, he said, is capable of anything. He's jealous, but there's something else.

Ibrahim had tried to explain to him. He told Tareq about me and how we'd met. He thought that opening up to Tareq would bring them closer, but it was a lost cause. "You've chosen your camp" was his cousin's only reply.

"So the telephone calls and the weird guys following you: is that Tareq's doing?"

Ibrahim pretended to ignore my question. Again he said that the only hope is his mother. She's the only one Tareq still listens to.

Jerusalem, April 7, 2009

I found the envelope on the doormat tonight when I came home after class. No address, just my name in capital letters.

I opened the envelope and unfolded the paper. Four letters spelled out "ZONA," the Hebrew word for whore.

I heard Ibrahim come into my room. He approached me slowly without looking at my face. He took me in his arms but I couldn't stop shaking.

❄

From: Sara
To: Daniel
Subject: News
Wednesday, April 8, 2009, 1:29 a.m.
Good evening, Papa.
I'm sorry I haven't called you. Don't worry.
I love you so much.
Sara

❄

When Samira arrived at Daniel's room for their daily meeting, she was greeted by a policeman who refused to let her in. At the end of the hall, she saw Detective Ben-Ami conferring with hotel personnel. She walked toward them. Ben-Ami recognized her and took her aside.

"You're Sara's friend, right?"

"Yes."

"I have bad news. We've found her body."

"Her—"

"Yes, dead. Throat cut. Her friend, Ibrahim Awad, as well. Both of them with their throats cut."

"Where?"

"In an apartment, in Haifa. We've told Sara's father. The funeral is tomorrow."

※

Samira wandered the streets late into the night. At first, she felt nothing. In her head, nothing but questions. Could it have been Tareq? Feeling that Ibrahim had humiliated and betrayed him, he could have tracked them down in Haifa. He could have hidden in their apartment, waited until they came home in the evening and then attacked them. Or maybe it was Avner. He, too, could have followed them. Could he have gotten an old army buddy to commit the murders for him? But soon the questions would evaporate and Samira would think only of Sara's father and his pain. Fear would overwhelm her. She would be afraid to see him again, afraid of not finding the words, afraid of being unable to meet his gaze. She would be afraid of no longer being present, of having already vanished from his sight.

※

From: Daniel
To: Sara
Subject: News
Thursday, April 9, 2009, 8:42 a.m.

160

Dearest Sara,

Thanks for your message. I noticed that it was after 1 a.m. when you sent it. Don't worry, I'm sure your exams will go well. Just send me a little "hey, Papa" when you have a minute.

I miss you and am thinking of you.

Papa

✻

Jerusalem, April 9, 2009

Ibrahim doesn't want me to call the police. He didn't say so, but I don't think he wants to cause trouble for Tareq. If the police get involved, Tareq might go to prison, even if he's innocent.

✻

Jerusalem, April 10, 2009

I had dinner with Tamar at the university café. I hardly ate a thing.

Tamar did her best to reassure me. She offered to talk to Avner for me. She'll question him discreetly. She can learn more from his answers and find out if he's really behind all this.

Maybe she's right. But I'm afraid that these attempts won't get us anywhere. Since we spilt up, I've seen Avner in a new light. Agreeable, friendly, kind, and then suddenly he gets impatient and flies into a massive rage the second he doesn't get his way. I can easily picture him playing the innocent. If Tamar questions him, he'll pretend that he doesn't have any idea what she's talking about, that he isn't aware of any of this, that he turned that page ages ago. But who knows what he is really capable of?

Jerusalem, April 11, 2009

I didn't tell Papa anything. When he calls, I talk only about my exams and the weather.

He'll be in Israel in a little over a month. I can't wait.

I'll introduce him to Samira and Ibrahim. I won't have to explain anymore. He'll be here with me, and right away, he'll understand.

Jerusalem, April 13, 2009, 9:15 p.m.
Another envelope. Inside, a sheet of white paper, folded into eight squares. "KALVA." BITCH.

This time, I'd had enough. After my classes, I went to the police station. The officer looked at the two pieces of paper on his desk. He looked up at me and gave me what he hoped was a reassuring smile. "I can see how this might be very unpleasant. But these aren't threats."

Not threats! Exactly what does he want? They're anonymous letters, right? And what about the obsessive phone calls that stop only when I turn my cell phone off? And the people following Ibrahim in the street?

But I was too furious to answer him. I picked up the letters, grabbed my knapsack and left.

On my way out of the stationhouse, I noticed a sky-blue Corolla parked across the street. I started to walk in the opposite direction and after a long detour, I made it to the bus stop. When I got off the bus at the Mount Scopus stop, I could have sworn that I saw the same car, a blue Toyota with a cracked windshield. I ran toward my building without looking back and rushed to my room.

Ibrahim still hasn't returned. I left him several messages but he hasn't called back. I really need him here with me.

Jerusalem, April 13, 2009, 10:45 p.m.
Ibrahim finally came back. He didn't tell me right away what had happened.

His hair a mess, out of breath, his forehead covered in sweat: I'd never seen him in such a state. His eyes roamed all over the room as if he were convinced that an intruder was hiding somewhere, ready to jump on him at any moment. He went over to the window, peeked through the curtains and stared into the darkness. He ignored all my questions.

Finally, he turned to look at me. "They… they… followed me." Who are "they"? But he just shrugged his shoulders and continued pacing. Then as if he'd just heard my question, "It was… it was them… the guys… in the bl… the bl… the blue car."

❄

Daniel was standing facing Sara's grave. A small group of men pressed around him like a flock that surrounds a newborn lamb to protect it from predators. Samira watched them from a distance.

She listened to Daniel's monotone voice, a distant voice sliding far, far beyond pain, like the reassuring words of a soldier sending new troops to the front. It was the *Kaddish*, the prayer for the dead. God exalted by men because nothing remained but the poverty of the living, the narrow path of their insignificance.

On her way out of the cemetery, Samira followed the short procession of Sara's cousins, friends and acquaintances. With head bent to avoid his eyes, each one in turn approached Daniel and said the same inaudible words, "I wish you long life." Samira also repeated the set phrases but couldn't help thinking that a long life without the two women he'd loved the most was probably the last thing Daniel wanted.

Daniel looked at her as if she were a stranger. In his eyes, almost nothing human remained. There was only a mineral whiteness, the organic indifference of a living thing observing another living thing.

Finally, Daniel took her hand. At this contact, he closed his eyes. Then his face brightened and in the smile formed by his pale, chapped lips, Samira saw that he had also recognized her pain.

❄

Jerusalem, April 18, 2009
Ibrahim's friend Elie is leaving to spend a month in New York and
is letting us use his apartment in Haifa. We leave tonight.

Haifa, April 20, 2009
I'm breathing a bit easier. For the first time in 15 days, I slept
almost peacefully.
    This morning, Ibrahim went out to buy bread and fruit. We
spent the day reading and listening to music. From time to time,
Ibrahim went to the window and looked at the street through the
blinds, then came back to sit next to me, looking relieved.
    Yet the fear is always there. The slightest breeze against the
window, the slightest noise outside the door, and I jump.

❈

Samira looked at Daniel, slumped in the armchair in his room.
He avoided her eyes but he was aware of her presence there. He was
afraid to be alone. When she got ready to leave, he would try to
make her stay.

❈

Haifa, April 21, 2009
We don't talk much. When he holds me in his arms, behind his
tenderness, there's the sterile fear that we'll be separated, as if a part
of ourselves has already been ripped from the other. We are nothing
more than memories, two shadows frozen in their embrace,
inseparable, pushed away again by the future.

Haifa, April 22, 2009
Again I asked Ibrahim, "Are you sure it's Tareq?" He shrugged his
shoulders. Then after a long silence, as if his voice was keeping pace
with his inner monologue, "I don't recognize him anymore. We were

*so close. Too close, maybe. I never wanted to hurt him, but he started
to hate me. He let them pollute his mind with all those hateful ideas.
When you get to that point, you're capable of anything..."*

I told him about Avner, our last encounter and what he'd said,
the words so full of resentment. Ibrahim didn't seem surprised. He
gave me a look that I know was meant to be comforting. The vibrant
gleam in his eyes had faded to a peaceful light. He sat down beside
me and let me lay my head on his chest. His pale hands covered my
face. "Eventually he'll forget. Jealousy always ends up forgetting."
He said it as would a professor stating a theorem. But deep down,
I knew full well that he didn't believe it.*

Haifa, April 23, 2009
*We've been here for five days. This morning, for the first time, we
went out together. After a long walk, we sat on the terrace of a café
on Hanassi Avenue.*

*When he saw how nervous I was, Ibrahim began to talk about
his memories of school, Haifa's parks where he'd played soccer with
his friends, the ups and downs of his friendship with Elie. I nodded
my head to show I was paying attention, but I couldn't stop looking
around, certain that we were being watched.*

❧

Samira's voice was scarcely audible, as if she were afraid to break
the silence's delicate balance. She had spoken to Detective Ben-
Ami. The investigation was progressing.

Daniel wanted to answer her but his thoughts took him back to
the last conversation he'd had with Sara, a week before his arrival in
Israel. Her voice had been more hesitant than usual. She'd seemed
distracted and had been evasive when answering his questions.
Then just before they hung up, out of the blue, there'd been that
rush of words, spoken as if they might burn her tongue: "I love you,
Papa." Sara normally ended their conversations by saying "See you

soon" or "Big kiss" or even the very American "Take care." At the time, Daniel had been surprised, but he soon thought no more about it. Only now did the words come back to him, not as a message of love but as a menacing and sinister sign. "I love you, Papa" meant, "I'm scared, I don't know what to do, I don't know what's going to happen to us."

☼

Haifa, April 24, 2009, 11:30 a.m.
This morning, I woke up before you. I watched you sleep, fascinated by your calm, regular breathing and its indifference to threats and fear. I kissed your forehead. Just then, you turned your head. Your eyelids contracted as if trying to hold on to the vanishing light, and I wondered what had become of my kiss when it was absorbed into your dreams.

Then you opened your eyes and I immediately started talking to chase away my dark thoughts.

"I dreamed about you again. It's always the same scene, more or less: I'm being chased by two huge brown dogs. I run and run, desperately. They bark, they growl, they're gaining ground. The streets are deserted. I call for help but no one hears me. At the end of the street, there's a wall. That's it; it's over. I stop and turn around. The dogs are no more than a few metres away from me. I look up and suddenly I see you, standing in the doorway of a house on one side of the narrow street. You look at me and see my terror. The dogs have surrounded me. They paw the ground, they fix me with their fierce, beady eyes. They're ready to leap, they're already salivating, snarling with fangs bared. And all the while, you remain impassive. You could call them, throw rocks at them or take a stick and smash their skulls. But you don't move. And weird as it may seem, it's a great comfort to know you're there. I could – I should – be angry at you. I should yell at you, "Do something! Make them go away!" But I don't feel the need. You're powerless and for that very reason, I'm not angry. Just

knowing that you see me is enough to calm me down. I am numb with fear but I feel confident. It's the end and I cannot see beyond that moment, yet all that matters is your presence, your infinitesimal and evanescent presence."

"Then what?"

"Then nothing. I wake up."

"I'm ha... happy to be in your... dreams. E... even if I almost d... d... don't exist."

"My father used to dream about my mother a lot. In the morning, when he would tell her about their nighttime adventures, she would smile as if she recognized the scenes he'd described, as if she'd actually been with him. He used to say, sounding like someone who's had a great deal of experience with life, that when you stop dreaming about your significant other, it's a sign that love has begun to go sour.

You took my hand and gave me a sorrowful look that seemed to say, "We may not have time to reach that point."

⁂

A blue notebook lay on the desk in the hotel room that Daniel had occupied since arriving in Israel. It was a student's notebook whose twisted metal rings made it difficult to turn the pages. Elie, Ibrahim's friend, had brought it to him. "I found it on the floor near the living room window before the police got to my place." He had leafed through it quickly. The pages were covered with fine writing, with curved letters adorned with generous loops. He'd recognized a few French words and realized it must have belonged to Sara.

Soon Daniel would rise from his armchair. He would open the notebook as if it were a precious manuscript. He would read the first words: *"My father is Jewish. My mother is Muslim. I am both. I've lived a long time without asking myself any questions."*

At first he would tell himself, "The solution is here, pointless to look any further. All I have to do is read and everything will become clear."

✳

From: Sara
To: Daniel
Subject: Don't worry

Friday, April 24, 2009, 7:25 p.m.
Just a quick note, Papa, to tell you everything is okay. Can't wait to
see you.
I love you.
Sara

✳

Haifa, April 25, 2009, 2:11 a.m.
That's it. It started again. I can't take this anymore.

Haifa, April 25, 2009, 10:08 a.m.
Last night and again this morning, a text message on my phone:
"ZONA." How did they get my number? Do they know I'm here? I
ran to the window. Could they be in the building across from us?
  Ibrahim hasn't come back yet.
  Why are they harassing us? "It's only to scare us. Eventually they'll
give up." Every day, Ibrahim tries to reassure me. But does he really
believe that?

Haifa, April 25, 2009, 11:30 p.m.
Another message. I turned my phone off.

Haifa, April 26, 2009
We bought tickets this morning. In two days, we leave for Montreal.
At least there they'll leave us alone.
  We'll stay as long as it takes, until they forget about us.

＊

For over three hours, Daniel sat motionless and buried himself in Sara's journal. He frantically turned the pages, seeking out any and all clues. He lingered on a passage about himself, went back to a page where Sara had reported one of their conversations, then skimmed the rest, slowing down only when the names Avner and Tareq appeared. The threats, the anonymous letters – the answer was there, it had to be. Soon, he would know, he was certain of it, and he would be able to call Detective Ben-Ami to tell him, "Call off the search, I know who did it."

＊

Haifa, April 27, 2009
We have nothing left to eat. Ibrahim went down to buy bread and fruit. I tried to keep him from going but he insisted. He promised to come back quickly.

After I closed the door, I went over to the window. I saw him open the gate and then disappear around the corner. A few minutes later, a blue car stopped right across from our building. I'm pretty sure it was a Corolla. Two men got out. They turned toward the fruit store. They went striding down the street, full of purpose.

Did they follow Ibrahim? No, maybe it's only a coincidence, my imagination running wild. There are plenty of blue Corollas...

I'm scared. Ibrahim still isn't back and he's been gone more than 20 minutes...

Again he made me promise not to call the police. But I'm too scared. I'm giving him two more minutes. If he's not back by then, I'm calling...

＊

From: Daniel
To: Sara
Subject: Answer me right away
Thursday, April 30, 2009, 11:08 p.m.

Sara, dear,
I've been trying to call you for several days. I left you several messages. Why aren't you answering? I'm worried. Please, please
answer me. Just send me a text just to say you're okay.
Your father who loves you

❄

*"I'm scared. Ibrahim still isn't back and he's been gone more than
20 minutes..."*

*"Again he made me promise not to call the police. But I'm too
scared. I'm giving him two more minutes. If he's not back by then, I'm
calling..."*

Those were the last words in Sara's journal. What had happened
after she'd written them? Who had entered that room before she'd
had time to call the police?

The questions droned in Daniel's head.

❄

Tucked into Sara's notebook, Daniel discovered pages written in
Hebrew and bearing as titles the names of biblical characters: Abraham, Job, Jacob... They were Ibrahim's stories, the ones he used to
read to Sara at night, to assuage her fear. Soon it would be Daniel's
turn to read them. Through these tales, he would try to get close to
his daughter, to retrace the steps back down a path that had, perhaps, helped her to be at peace with herself.

❄

"We're almost there. Another couple of days and we'll have the perpetrator," said Detective Ben-Ami. Daniel hung up, looked at Samira and walked toward the window that overlooked the hotel parking lot.

The young woman finally convinced him to leave his room. She led him to the elevator. Docilely, Daniel followed her to the restaurant.

Samira kept looking at his face, hoping that he would look back at her. She wanted him to understand, without her having to say it, that she would not leave, that she would stay by his side, however long it might take.

She noticed his forehead, furrowed with deep wrinkles resembling the sinuous paths that the ocean carves into the sand. Below his eyes, heavy grey bags had formed. His cheeks had caved inward so that the whiteness of bone showed beneath his translucent skin. Only the mouth held on to a bit of his former life and when he smiled, his features regained their serenity.

Soon they would know. And afterwards? Daniel would return to Montreal. He would have to find the strength to go on, to rebuild. Although he didn't talk about Sara's death, Samira thought she knew what he was thinking: going on meant accepting a new life, being born into a world where Sara no longer existed. What was the point of a future if it was no longer for Sara that everything would begin anew?

But Daniel wasn't thinking about death. He wasn't thinking about anything at all. He looked at Samira and all he saw were her amber eyes, eyes that seemed to tremble like water just before it comes to a boil, like the sand that slowly trickles from the palm of our hand.

❄

In Daniel's hotel room, the sun's first rays cast a pale, damp light on the walls. It was 6 o'clock in the morning. Samira, stretched out in the armchair, was awakened by a murmuring. A language that sounded like Hebrew or Arabic.

Yit-gadal v'yit-kadash sh'may rabbah... Standing with his face turned toward the window and a prayer book in his hands, Daniel was reading the words of the *Kaddish*. The words poured out, each one a birth, each birth the memory of her absence: Sara's death, a thousand times repeated.

B'almah di-v'rah chiru-tai... Daniel, who for weeks had lived on nothing but his memory, could no longer abide having only that to bring him closer to Sara. Before, he had managed to tolerate the recollections of past joys because Sara, alive, could give him new ones. But his daughter's death had made his memory responsible for the entire future, for all the untested truths he had left to live. His memories, those pale, paltry vassals made to bear alone the crown of life? He despised them and wanted to eliminate them from his mind. Because they had betrayed him. Because they cruelly reminded him of the face that had bound him to life while they, those pitiful phantoms, were incapable of sustaining the life belonging to that face.

V'yam-lich mal-chutai... Daniel grieved with each phrase, but it hardly mattered. That prayer, those words in Aramaic, would henceforth bear the memory that never stops growing, like a rising tide, the memory of a present where Sara is absent, a memory burdened with a future robbed of life. He grieved because he was alone. He grieved with anger and fury. He grieved this death, this violence and this hate. He grieved because he didn't understand and no longer wanted to understand.

V'yatz-mach purkanai v'karaiv m'shi-chai... But Daniel, the man who did not know God, conscientiously recited this prayer, each word calling for the next, opening a new passage into an uninhabited future.

B'chai-yai-chon uv'yo-may-chon... This prayer was sent to explore the new world that awaited him, a place with no past, no words, no refuge, a life with gaping holes, mended, reassembled, a life where every object would signal Sara's absence and where every look would mean, "I don't know her, I never met her."

Uv-cha-yai d'chowl bait Yisrael... A fragment of a memory of Sara was attached to each word. He had to go to the very end, to the final "amen," and then, perhaps, the image would be complete.

Ba-agala u'vi-zman ka-riv, v'imru amen... These words were a path. It was enough to continue, to say another word and another and another, and during that time, life – murmur and hum – slipped in behind him and pulled him along while he wasn't looking. These words called him and carried him. Already, the next day was dawning in them. These words called him and protected him and led him away from the pain.

✳

Daniel put down the prayer book and turned toward Samira. On his face, stripped of emotion and desire after these weeks of torment, there was only fear. Fear of being abandoned; fear of having to bear, far into the future, an immense and barren past; the fear, perhaps, of not being able to face a world lying fallow where everything had yet to be built.

But was this distress already sheltering, in its silence and its perseverance, the shadow of a beginning?

WHEN THE FATHER KNEELS ON THE SAND, the son approaches and faces his father, head bent toward the ground.

For a long time, Abraham's hands travel over his son's cheeks, lips and eyelids, as if trying to hold on to the life that was escaping. His fingers will remember this face long after its death, this face at the confluence of so many desires, unsuspected hopes and fervent trust.

Isaac raises his head and looks at his father, but his father's gaze is lost somewhere beyond the mountain. Only his lips are moving.

Surely it's a prayer, a prayer that Isaac does not know.

But Abraham's words do not sing praises.

"My God, look at me! Look at my hand! Soon the knife in its grasp will bear down on the neck of my son, my only son, the son I love, the son I dreamt of for so long.

"My God, answer me! I must hear the voice that does not come from within my own heart!

"My God, turn your face to me! So that I can finally know your presence!"

Abraham raises the knife, ready to strike. His hand does not tremble, but from his half-open lips escapes a feverish whisper, like a scream from within.

"My God, stay my hand! Show me that you are more than my life and that I am not alone in this existence to which I am exiled.

"If you are master of this world, you would not allow a man to take from his son the very life that you have given him.

"If you are something other than my dream, your hand will meet mine and I will know, even if you must withdraw from the world forever, that this one time we will have been two, you the infinite observer and I, the man who sees you."

Abraham's lips twist into a monstrous grimace. His wide-open eyes turned toward the sun, he hears only his own breathing, broken by the howling wind.

His fingers tighten again around the handle of the knife; his arm stiffens. But before dealing the blow, he looks at Isaac's head.

It is then that he sees his son's face as if for the very first time.

In the naked pallor of Isaac's expression, there is neither fear nor reproach. His face speaks only of love and trust.

Abraham's hand begins to tremble. This being that he wanted to remove from the world was slowly bringing him back to life.

Isaac, flesh of his flesh, was no longer his son; he was the child of man, the stranger who calls to him and to whom he responds. God has no other face but this.

Abraham drops the knife. He puts his fevered hands over Isaac's eyes, as if to protect them from the light.

In the now-peaceful silence, Abraham studies the horizon.

The voices have withdrawn. They may never come again. But what need has he of signs when he has before him the other man's miracle?

In Isaac's eyes, there are no more questions. He exists, immense, a lone pillar before the solitude of Abraham.

The father finally closes his burning eyes.

He features are changing. A peace as warm as a morning cloud spreads through his aching body.

He pulls his son toward him and enfolds him a long embrace.

SOURCES OF QUOTATIONS IN ORDER OF APPEARANCE IN THE BOOK

Elon, Amos. *Jerusalem: Battlegrounds of Memory*.

Darwish, Mahmoud. "In Jerusalem." Translated from the Arabic by Fady Joudah. http://www.poetryfoundation.org/poem/236752

Khoury, Elias. *Gate of the Sun*.

Stoppard, Tom. *Rosencrantz and Guildenstern Are Dead*. New York, Grove Press.

Ibsen, Henrik. *Ibsen Plays: Five: Brand and Emperor and Galilean*. Translated and introduced by Michael Meyer. Great Britain, Methuen London Ltd.

Darwish, Mahmoud. "Tuesday and the Weather Is Clear." Translated from the Arabic by Fady Joudah. http://www.poetrysociety.org.uk/lib/tmp/cmsfiles/File/review/Darwish.pdf

Hillesum, Etty. Quotation from Alexandra Pleshoyano's "Etty Hillesum: For God and with God," in which the author cites as the source of the translation *Etty: The Letters and Diaries of Etty Hillesum, 1941-1943*, edited by Klaas A.D. Smelik, translated by Arnold J. Pomerans (Ottawa: Novalis, 2002).